HIS TO SAVE

NW EARTH
BOOK THREE

SELINA COFFEY
SUMMER COOPER

LOVY BOOKS

The low rumble of thunder shook the ground and Ann looked up, disoriented. Where was Rager, she worried. Where were the guards that should have been here to protect them both?

Rager wasn't there, he'd gone… somewhere. Confusion muddled her brain into a thick sludge that would not allow for coherent thoughts. Someone had come for her, she remembered. A voice came out of the darkness, a voice that had made her run to the back of the secret room she'd been hiding in.

She'd tripped and fallen to the ground, as she ran from the anger, the venom, in that voice.

"Ann! Get off your ass and come with me. Now!" Rex's voice, filled with excited anger, shouted at her over the din of the battle that continued in the distance.

She remembered now. Rex.

Rex's voice had come from the darkness and filled her with terror as he proclaimed he was about to kill her child and take her with him to do... something. She didn't want to know what. She'd blocked it out for a moment, all of it. Her fear of him, of where Rager had disappeared to, and her anger at Rex, because deep down she knew, she absolutely knew, he'd caused this.

She knew she didn't have time to act the simpering maiden in need of a savior, she had to protect herself, and her baby, from this absolute idiot. If that meant following his orders, so be it. For now.

She pushed herself off the ground, wiped at her bottom to remove any dust, and stood tall to look at Rex. Always the pest, this little bastard, always the one that caused problems. For now, she would do as he said, after all, he carried with him the weapons of the aliens and she knew he hated her now.

She knew that it wasn't just that he hated her, he loathed her. But not because she'd done anything to him personally. Well, not really. He'd decided he wanted her when the world came back to life, and that she could be his new toy. Only his toy turned out to be the mate of the aliens he detested. Now, carrying the child of an alien, she wasn't just a traitor in his mind, she was polluted goods.

"Katy," she called into the darkness, where Katy had run to when the door opened.

"Leave your fucking dog, Ann. We can't take that mongrel with us. It's too damn yappy." Rex barked the words at her, and she turned away, stunned at his cruelty. Although, she thought, by this point, she shouldn't be.

With a tilt of her chin, Ann followed along behind Rex, determined to do whatever it took to stay safe, to protect her child. Hopefully, someone at the house would take care of the puppy for her. She didn't want to leave her, but with the mood Rex was in, it was probably best to keep her away from him.

He was dressed in black cargo pants and a black t-shirt with a wolf howling at the moon printed on the front. The uniform of the new army of the revolutionaries, the wolves and other malcontents. She would have found him handsome in the past, with his blond hair and hazel eyes, standing tall with triumph. Now, she saw him for what he was.

An asshole that didn't want anyone else to play with his toys.

"Where is your transporter?" he asked, but it was more a demand for information than a polite question.

"Outside." She nudged her chin in the direction of the front door and walked behind him. She was glad now that she'd dressed when this all started, even if it was stuff she'd thrown on in the darkness. She didn't feel naked at least, as they made their way through the destroyed house.

She scanned the rooms with furtive glances but did not see Rager or any of the people that should have been there. She didn't even see bodies, but then, the place was a wreck now. It was possible there were bodies…

Ann stumbled behind Rex and crossed her arms over her stomach. She would not think the worse, she just wouldn't. Rager was somewhere out there, otherwise, she'd know it. She would feel it. Wouldn't she?

"Fuck, when did you get so clumsy, Ann? Keep up, or I'll shoot you now and get this all over with." Rex's face was a mask of hate that Ann could not look at.

She kept her gaze on the ground and walked out of the door. She walked into the transporter, Rex close behind, and put her hands on the controls. The transporter responded to her touch, as it always did, and began to hover over the ground.

"How far can we get in this thing?" Rex asked from the seat beside her.

"It can cross the entire globe, indefinitely. It runs on an energy I don't quite understand. It's not really fuel…" her words faltered as she tried to think of how to explain it. "It's not like our combustible engines, it's a technology we don't have. Not perpetual motion, but something like that."

"That doesn't make any sense, Ann," Rex complained

and kicked his feet out in front of his body as he slouched in his seat, his weapon aimed right at her. "You never were the brightest lightbulb in the pack, I have to say."

Ann didn't rise to his bait, she just pushed the transporter to leave the vicinity of the house, without a real direction in mind. She just knew that if she followed his orders, and got him far away from Rager, then she might be able to ensure that her new little family would all survive this night.

"Head east, away from this place. I'm finished with these people now."

So, she thought, he's started a revolution just to get what he wanted. Rex always had been a rather stupid boy, and he'd just proven it with this stunt. She'd wondered about it for a long time, what his ultimate goal was with this drive to start a revolution. She'd thought he wanted to rule the entire world, but as it turned out, he just wanted to ruin her.

Talk about not being the brightest lightbulb in the pack!

Once his cronies figured out he'd abandoned them, they would probably come after him. Or assume he was lost in battle somewhere, though she doubted he'd actually had anything to do with the fighting. He probably sat back while the others all fought their way into the

Overlord's house, and then came in as it finished. That was more his style.

What he didn't seem to grasp, even at this very moment, was that the aliens were not only more powerful, they actually controlled all of the planet. This whole affair was an effort in futility, but as always, Rex was too stupid to see the big picture. All he could see was what he wanted.

Sure, the idea of a revolution was a good one, especially when he'd only orchestrated the whole thing to get to her, but that was typical of Rex. He'd pull out some brilliant nugget of intelligence, but then he'd fuck it all up somewhere along the way. If she played it smart, did as he told her, and waited for her chance, she could escape this entire fiasco.

Then she'd find her way back to Rager, and they'd find somewhere safe to have this baby. Her free hand moved as she aimed the transporter in the vague direction of the east. She cradled the place where her baby grew and promised that she would find a way out of this that was safe for them both.

She hadn't wanted to be the Overlord's mate, she hadn't asked for it, or competed for his attention. He'd made that decision long before she even met him. She'd dreamed about him, and now he was real. He was a part of her, a part she didn't want to lose. She was only calm because their connection let her know that he was still alive.

"What are you doing?" Rex asked with a snip of anger in his voice.

"I'm touching my stomach," she said softly, without any inflection at all. She knew she had to keep Rex calm, for now at least.

"Stop that. You shouldn't be cradling that filth you have in there. I'm going to take care of that as soon as we get to where we're going."

"Where might that be?" Ann kept her gaze on the dark scenery ahead of her. She kept up a mantra in her head as she did so. Don't provoke him, don't provoke him.

"I haven't decided yet." He looked away from her, back out to the forest on the ground below.

Ann ignored the words he'd said, about her baby being filth and the rest of it. He was obviously off his rocker, and the only way she would get out of this was to think ahead, stay calm, and try not to antagonize him.

She wanted nothing more than to go back home, to climb back into bed, and to wake up with the knowledge that this had all been a nightmare. Katy would be there, waiting for her to take her outside, and to play in the garden with her. Maybe if she just jumped up and punched the idiot, she could surprise him and knock him out.

She knew none of that would happen though, this was real, and heroics or antagonizing Rex wouldn't win the day. She knew the heroine always talked back in the films, she always got away after some witty comment, but real life was different.

The newspapers used to be full of reports about women that were kidnapped and murdered. Life in general seemed to lose some kind of meaning before the end of the world came. Road rage had been an actual thing. People killed each other because of... driving. Because of songs. Because of sports teams. Because it was Wednesday and a good day to lose your mind.

It was all ridiculous really, how life lost its value. Ann knew she'd been sheltered in many ways, but she had the same access to the news media that everybody else had. She'd seen it on her computer screen, heard her friends talk about it, seen it on the television. And now, Rex wanted to continue that devaluation of life and kill her baby, and maybe even her. Because of a few genetic differences.

Anger flooded into her veins, but not the reckless kind that had driven so many in the world before the end came. No, this was a calm kind of anger, the kind that helped her to see clearly, that allowed her to wait. With a slight tilt of her head, Ann began to wait, and to watch, for any mistake Rex made.

He was Rex, after all, star-studded, All-American

boy-goodness, so full of himself he was certain he was the only one good enough, smart enough, to rule the day. Ann knew better, though, and so she waited.

"What are you doing?" Rex asked when she lowered the altitude of the transporter.

"There's a storm ahead, I thought it would be safer to stay close to the ground."

"Oh. Well. Tell me before you do something like that next time." He curled up in his chair like a little boy settled into the couch on a cold, rainy day. All he needed was a blanket and his mommy there to bring him a sandwich and a hot drink.

The image burned into her mind, a portrait of Rex's cowardly childishness that told her she would get out of this mess, and that she would find Rager. Somehow.

For a moment, Ann wondered if Rex would turn into a wolf anytime soon. Was it his time of the month? Or had he got that out of the way before he tried to destroy her world? She didn't want to have to deal with Rex in his wolf shape.

Before the end came, she'd always assumed wolves were dog-sized, not too big, maybe the size of a German shepherd, but no bigger. After the end came, she'd seen how big he was. He was big, bigger than his parents, and ferociously feral, even after he'd become used to the process. His parents had become tame versions of their animal selves. Not Rex. He wasn't a threat to them, but if anyone else had come around, he might have been.

And now? Now that she was his enemy, would he see her as a threat? She thought he might. She watched him, but he didn't show any of the signs that came before a shift. He wasn't fidgeting or full of the nervous energy that would cause him to twitch sometimes. He was always a little hyper, and certainly aggressive, but he didn't seem... frenetic, as he was before a shift.

For now, she seemed to be safe from that, at least. She tried not to think any further than that. To do so would just cause her to panic. When a stray thought would try to slip through, she'd move around in her seat, roll her head on her neck, or just change the point in the distance that she gazed at.

The sun had started to rise, and the sky began to glow with the coming dawn. She watched as the miles passed below them, curious about what the world looked like now. It didn't appear to have changed much, but she knew she should have passed much more desert than she had. Instead, she'd seen rivers and streams, forests where none should have been. It must have been the doings of the aliens, this renewed life.

"Where are we?" Rex asked and made Ann jump. She thought he'd fallen asleep, but quite obviously, he hadn't.

"Somewhere over Nevada, I think. It might be New Mexico, I'm not sure." The aliens had tried to recreate a navigational system but hadn't been able to recreate the system that humans had before the end came. She couldn't read the system they'd replaced it with.

"That sounds about right." He got up from his seat and walked around the transporter.

She heard a door open and then the sound of water being poured from a plastic container. She would have liked some but didn't want to ask him for anything. Not when it would just come with a snotty reply or a refusal.

She glanced at the weapon he'd left in his seat but knew she wouldn't be able to reach it before he made it back to the chair. It wasn't worth the risk, not yet. For now, it was best to wait for a better opportunity. Rex would offer her one, she had no doubt about that at all. She could always count on him to screw up somewhere along the way.

"Do you want a drink?" he asked and handed her a small cup of water.

She took the offered drink with a murmured thanks before she handed the cup back. He went back to the cupboard and put the cup away.

"You know he's dead, right?" He'd come up right behind her as he asked the question, and Ann tensed. "Your alien lover and all of his cronies will be little more than carrion by now. There's nothing for you to go back to. So, don't worry your pretty little head about things like escaping, alright? You have nowhere to go now. My men will assume I've died, your family will think you've gone missing or have died as well, and nobody will look for you. Get used to that idea now and we'll have fewer problems. Understood?"

"Yes, Rex," she said softly, without turning to look at him. Her toes curled on the floor and that was the only sign she gave of how much she wanted to beat him to death with a shoe.

2

He growled low in his throat as he gave off a volley of blue death with his weapon. The sound of a pained scream filled the air and he knew whoever it was that had followed him would follow no more. With one final glance back, he made his way to the location of the ground-to-ship transporters, the kind that moved him from the ground back up to his spaceship.

"I want soldiers down there, now, Raya," he said as he appeared on the ship, the atoms of his body still cementing back together as he spoke.

A voice filled the air and spoke in the language of his people. It was a feminine voice, designed to soothe and calm. The computer that operated the systems on the ship was able to listen for any command from any of his people on the ship and respond.

"Yes, Overlord. Do you want to destroy all of the humans or just those involved in this insurrection?"

Rager thought about the last image he had of Ann, her face as he closed the panel that should have kept her safe. Someone had informed the revolutionaries about the safe room, though, because Ann had been taken. He'd seen it for himself when he went back to the house.

"Only the revolutionaries that will not submit, Raya." He marched from the transport room and in the direction of the command station. "Otherwise, I want them found and interrogated. I want to know where Ann is. After that, I'll decide on what to do with them. Hold them after they are questioned until I say otherwise."

On his planet, caution was taken, and one was encouraged to make full use of every item available. To kill all of the revolutionaries would have been stupid, meaningless, and might encourage others to join the cause. If he kept them prisoner, wrung out every bit of information they could give, and left them for a while, he might find some other use for them.

Plus, Ann had started new thoughts in his head. Perhaps their system was unfair. That didn't mean that he thought the revolutionaries were right to stage an insurrection, it just meant that he might see matters from their point of view more than he'd realized. He sighed as he stepped heavily in the direction of the command center. This hadn't been easy, none of it, and now, the social structure they had created had proven to be a path for discontent in the sectors. Not a good thing.

He'd come to Earth with the idea in his mind that there had to be a hierarchy. People had to be in charge. Humans, even when they craved anarchy, always, always looked for a leader. That was the information they had about the planet. He'd given them what they needed, and still, they'd found a reason to be unhappy. Or some of them had.

He'd have to find a new way, then. That was a problem for later, though. Right now, he needed to focus on getting Ann back.

"Pull up the file on shifter number 02197."

The computer dinged to let him know it had acknowledged his command before it spoke again.

"I have the file, Overlord, what would you like to know?" The voice had not changed inflection, it was only relaying information, as it always did.

"Where is he taking Ann, Raya? Find them for me, now." He walked through the automatic door and onto the deck of the command center.

People rushed around him, terrified of his wrath, and eager to find his mate before any other of his people did. They didn't understand though, not what his true thoughts were, anyway.

He wasn't furious because they'd taken his child, he was furious because his mate had been taken. That's what truly mattered. He hadn't wanted to feel like this about her, had hated the idea of being mated, but his match had been found, well before he met her, and he'd had time to adjust to the idea. He wanted her in his life by the time she'd actually been brought to him. Now, he didn't want to live without her.

It was the child that should have mattered, repopulation of the planet with children of their lineage was vital to the plans set in place for this planet. That child didn't seem real to him, not yet, anyway. It was also the one thing his mind rebelled against.

He hadn't wanted a child, had never planned to have children. He'd known when he came to this planet that he would have to reproduce, it would be expected, then demanded, but he'd wanted to wait. He couldn't help it that his mate was the most attractive woman he'd ever encountered, and he'd bedded her far more times than was probably decent. He'd still… hoped that they would have more time together before a child came along.

Everyone on this ship thought it was the child that he was keen to retrieve, but in actuality, he really only cared about his mate. Though he'd never admit it out loud, he didn't want that baby, not yet. He knew it had disappointed Ann that he hadn't reacted with more enthusiasm than he had, but he couldn't pretend to be happy when they'd both been forced to create that baby.

The humans of this planet thought that the aliens of his people were emotionless, cruel even, to demand children from their mates. They didn't know that there were those amongst his people that hated the demand as much as the humans did. Not everyone felt the same way he and Ann did about their mate, after all. Not all of them wanted to breed, either. But it was not a choice given to any of them, and he'd have to face up to facts sooner or later.

Ann carried his child, and whether he liked it or not, that baby would come soon enough. Whether she liked it or not, too, he thought after a moment's contemplation.

"Overlord," the computer system prompted as Rager headed for the armory at the other side of the command station. "I have located your mate and have locked onto their signal."

"Thank you, Raya. Please have a transporter ready for me and a few soldiers."

"Overlord, we need you, now!" A call from his generals came through and he turned back to face a screen that appeared on the wall.

"I've given Raya my instructions. What else do you need to know?"

"There are fires all over your sector, Overlord, and injured everywhere. Should we bring medical teams down here or just send the injured up to the ship? What about the fires? The fire crews are working all out, but the fires keep popping up."

"Damn!" Rager cursed and turned away from the screen. He wanted to go after his mate, to throttle that arrogant little prick, Rex, and bring her back to safety, but his people needed him.

Earthling and alien alike. With a growl of frustration and a swipe across his tired face, Rager turned back to the screen. "Get some soldiers and use the water from the reservoir nearby, don't use the seawater, it will only contaminate the ground. Get the injured up here, but set up a medical unit down there. I think there's a woman with a clinic down there now? Take the minor injuries to her."

Another call came in, the families that had been displaced by the bombs needed to be housed, where were they to put these now homeless people? Again and again, Rager's attention was dragged away to deal with some problem faced by the people below. He knew it was his duty, and he did it with care, but Ann needed him, their baby needed him. He owed it to his people, though, and to those back home that depended on him to lay the groundwork for those that would soon join his people on Earth.

It took hours to get all of the questions answered, and then he had to go back down and gather intel from his team questioning the prisoners that were taken. The head of the team met him in a small room inside a local jail that had been recommissioned after their arrival but hadn't been used yet.

"Tell me what you've learned, Elugon," Rager demanded as he sat down in a chair in one of the meeting rooms in the facility. He'd barely slept before the attack and he'd been on his feet for hours. He started to feel those hours now, as he sat down and looked across the table at the other man.

"Not a lot, Overlord. Most are tight-lipped still, but one has cracked. He speaks of a man out in the desert, but won't say his name or where in the desert this man is."

"I see." Rager studied Elugon, a very tall, intimidating man with shaggy black hair chopped into a short wreath around his head. The man's cold purple eyes didn't help to ease the ferocity of his gaze, rather, it added to it.

"I wish I did, Overlord. This is all utter nonsense. We could have taken their planet, filled it with our kind, and used them all as slaves, yet they protest? I would think they'd thank us."

"Thank us for turning them into slaves, Elugon? Oh, we haven't made them all slaves, not all of them, but most of them, yes. And we don't give them a single choice on breeding new children for the planet, either. No, we'd be wise to listen to their complaints, if we want to stay here and have them on our side. Otherwise, we will have to decimate the population, hunt them all down, and kill every last one of them. Call me crazy, but I think that would be impossible on this planet. Besides, our mandate is to repopulate and breed with the natives. Not destroy the entire population."

Normally, Rager would not have given such a long speech to someone under his command, but he had a feeling it was an argument he'd have to repeat many times, so if he practiced it on this leader, then he might have it perfect by the time he said it for the last time.

"Yes, Overlord. You are correct and far wiser than me, as always." Elugon bowed his head respectfully, and Rager frowned. He hadn't wanted to berate the man, but that's what it had turned into.

"It's not an easy thing to do, after all, is it, Elugon?" He put his hand on the other man's shoulder and squeezed. "This idea of renewing a planet and remaking it in an image we can admire."

"No, it's not, Overlord. Your burden is heavy. Especially with your mate and child missing." Elugon looked off beyond Rager's shoulder, his narrowed purple eyes dark. "We will bring them back to you."

"We will." He sighed and tried to remember what he'd been about to do before he'd come down to question Elugon. He couldn't keep track of what he'd done and hadn't done so far. "Thanks, Elugon. Keep at them and keep me informed."

"Yes, Overlord." Elugon stood up to open the door for Rager, but he'd already opened the door himself.

Rager nodded at the man and left the room. He headed back up to the ship, only to find people in chaos. Their supreme overlord had been attacked, his mate taken, and the sector was now in a contained chaos. The fighters would soon be dealt with, all of them, and order could be restored. But for now, soldiers ran back and forth with information, papers, maps, and instructions that needed to be relayed to dozens of other people.

"Selaira, what's the status on my mate's parents?" Rager asked a female soldier.

"They are in their home, as are the Wolfson servants. Do you want us to question them now about the fugitive?"

"No, once dawn has broken you can question them. For now, we know which direction the fugitive who has my mate is headed and there's a squad on the way out there to track them. He has one of our weapons, so I don't want any heroic attempts made at saving her. It might put her, or the team, in danger." Rager spoke softly, his voice an indication of his present turmoil. He still had a lot of work to do and not a lot of patience to get it all done.

He wanted to commandeer a transporter of his own, tell his people to solve the problems that continued to crop up on their own, and go after Rex and Ann. But he knew his people needed him to be their leader right now, just like the humans on this planet needed him to be their leader too.

He thought over the way he'd handled things in the last few hours as Selaira walked away and knew his mate had already influenced him. A few months ago, he'd have likely just had the fighters executed, and dealt with the flack from his home planet. Now, he understood the plight of the people on this world a little more, and knew he had to approach matters differently.

"Right, what's next on the list?" he called out to nobody in particular and a man stepped forward. He needed Rager to approve the use of their alien equipment to remove debris from a building that collapsed. People were trapped inside. Rager approved and moved on to the next task at hand.

Normally, his days were filled with activity, training, and a standard agenda of things that needed to be done. His people were edging out into countries all over the world now, and he had plans for each new place as his people discovered them. Today, however, would be about dealing with the mess in his own sector. He'd thought the humans would buckle under and go about the business of rebuilding. He hadn't dreamed they'd want to join forces with the shifters of the planet.

The shifters had killed a lot of people, long before the cold came. As temperatures dropped, a lot more people died, and that left the planet with a very small population. Wouldn't they want to work together to rebuild? It seemed most were willing to do that, and the shifters were contained now. They were tracked carefully to a precise moment when their shift was about to happen, and then they would be locked away from anyone they could harm. Still, there were those that thought they could overthrow the alien race that had invaded, resurrected, their planet and wanted to be some kind of post-apocalypse king.

He wouldn't be so complacent in the future. He wouldn't let humans destroy what should be a planet big enough for them all. Not on his watch.

3

"I need to pee," Rex complained, his voice wheedling and childish.

"Use the toilet then," Ann blurted out, her nerves frayed and her mind exhausted.

"No, that thing's disgusting!" He recoiled in his seat, as if she'd told him to drop himself down into an open-air sewer.

"It's just a hose, silly. And my back is turned." Not like she wanted to catch a glimpse of him anyway, she thought to herself. She'd used the thing before, with a cup adaptor, and no, it wasn't ideal, but it did the job when you needed to go and had no tree to hide behind.

"Just set the transporter down, stupid." Rex barked the order and she turned to look at him.

Her left eyebrow lifted but she didn't respond. It was pointless to argue with him; she knew that now. Rex lived in his own little make-believe world where he was the smartest living being on the planet, and he'd outfoxed everyone. Let him have his petty little snipes, she'd prove him wrong before long.

Ann looked around the area beneath them but there was only a giant lake for as far as she could see. Probably from the snow and ice that melted when the aliens came to save them all, she thought. They flew on for another couple of miles and then the horizon began to glow.

"What's that?" Rex barked out, like she was supposed to have an answer.

"I have no idea." She frowned, confused by the light. "A forest fire maybe?"

She could remember news reports about huge wild-fires spread around California in the years before the end came. They'd terrified her, given her nightmares, but she'd never come close to the fires, thankfully. Now, she wondered if they were about to fly over one. Would it damage the transporter?

"It's getting brighter," Rex mumbled and went back to his seat. "Maybe you should lift the transporter a little higher."

Ann didn't argue, she just brought the transporter up and waited, her breath held, until they came nearer to the glow.

"Higher!" Rex called urgently, fear in his voice. Ann couldn't blame him, her own heart thudded with terror as she began to see the cause of that demonic-looking light.

A giant rift had opened in the ground below, and somehow, unbelievably, the rift sucked down massive lava flows. It looked like a nightmare landscape, even from their higher altitude. Everywhere lava glowed, white, orange, a darkening black where some of the lava had cooled on top.

"Get us out of here, now!" Rex ordered with a sound very close to a whimper.

"I can't go any faster, the transporter just won't do it. I might be able to go around it." Ann headed for what she hoped was an edge as they passed miles and miles of lava flow.

"A volcano must have opened up, or maybe a caldera that was hidden became active again, or something." Ann tried to remember her lessons with Amanda, Rex's mother, about geology and what might have happened to the planet to cause the cataclysm.

"I don't know anything about volcanoes, or calderas, but I do know it looks like the entire continent has split in that rift down there." Rex's voice started to calm as they edged closer to darkness, the black edge of cool lava or no lava at all.

"I can't believe that's in our country. Sure, Hawaii has volcanoes, even super-volcanoes, if I remember correctly, but I didn't think we had anything like this."

She vaguely remembered something about Yellowstone National Park, but couldn't remember exactly what she'd read in the textbook. Maybe it had all been Yellowstone, she didn't know, but she did know there was a terrifying amount of lava down there.

It must have been terrible in this area when the rift opened, the fear people must have felt. She wondered if they'd had time to feel fear, though. If the rift had opened quickly enough, or if the lava had come first, out of somewhere, then maybe they'd died instantly. Hopefully, that had been the case she decided.

She'd like to know the full extent of the rift and the lava, but she had no idea if the transporter could withstand the kind of heat coming up off the ground down there. If there was actually ground left.

"I wonder if Hawaii is still there." Rex drew her attention back to him and she glanced at him.

"I doubt it. Between the volcanoes there, the earthquakes, tsunamis, and all the rest that must have happened, I doubt there's much that wasn't scoured away by something."

"I bet it made the place bigger, all of that stuff. Maybe sea levels have fallen, and the islands are more visible. I wonder..." Rex's voice trailed off for a moment, and she could all but see the wheel turning in his head. "I bet the entire geography of our world is different now. It would be interesting to see how it's changed."

"More land to be king of?" she snarked and regretted it instantly. She'd promised herself she wouldn't provoke him, and she'd done just that. She shot a glance at him out of the corner of his eye, but apparently, he hadn't heard her. She breathed a sigh of relief and drove on.

"I bet there's new land all over the place and lands that have disappeared. I wonder what global water levels are at now."

For a minute it almost sounded like he knew what he was talking about. Ann knew he'd been an average student, so he wasn't exactly stupid. Just a dick.

"You could be right," she replied and shifted around in her seat.

She'd been driving a very long time and her back, neck, and bottom were sore. The transporter would only respond to her or Rager, though, so it was impossible to let Rex drive. Not that she would anyway. That little bit of control kept her from totally losing her mind, right now. She wouldn't complain too much.

"I don't think it's safe to land anywhere near that lava. The black parts might still be hot, and the air is probably poisoned by gases." She ventured, remembering videos in long-ago science classes with volcanologists covered head to toe in protective gear as they walked on the black crust. "It might be safe, but I wouldn't want to take that chance."

"Oh, don't worry, I don't want to go down anywhere near that stuff. I'll hold it for a while longer." Rex settled back into his chair, crossed his legs, and went quiet.

Ann did what she'd done for what felt like hours now; she guided the transporter eastward. It wasn't hard to do, a gentle nudge on the joystick, a press of a button here and there. The hardest part was watching for objects she might crash into. A tree taller than the rest, a hill that came up of out nowhere suddenly. There'd been no buildings tall enough around here to cause a problem, but she doubted there would be many.

A rift like that must have caused quite a lot of damage throughout the country. It spread out for at least a mile, and the lava flows around had likely destroyed an entire state. The earthquakes that came with it must have moved mountains. Or produced the sudden hills she had to keep dodging.

She sighed, tense with Rex near, tired and sore from the events of the last few hours, and angry that she was helpless. She'd felt so safe with Rager as her mate, especially when she was near him. But Rex had made it clear that safety wasn't always something she could count on. He'd made it crystal clear, in fact.

For a moment, pure hatred filled her until it made her hands shake. He'd messed up everything, likely put both their parents in danger, and had threatened to kill her child. He'd been so vicious when he pulled her from that closet, she'd been terrified of him. Now that he was certain he'd escaped Rager, he thought he could relax. He didn't exude evil, and that almost lulled her into a false sense of security.

She knew better though. Rex was a snake, hidden in the grass, capable of a strike at any moment. To relax around him would be stupid.

She tried not to think about what must be happening with their parents. Rager would, hopefully, be lenient with both her and Rex's parents. For now, she tried to focus on an escape plan. She tried to think of what might be stowed in the transporter. There were no weapons other than the one he'd brought in with him, and she doubted there was much she could use. She wasn't a power-lifter or an expert in martial arts.

She'd have to outwit him, then. Make him believe she'd given in to her role as a captive and that his trauma-inducing speech when he'd first nabbed her had cowed her into obedience. Her brain screamed 'fuck that', but she didn't want him to know it. She just drove on.

Minutes passed, Rex began to tap his fingers against the arms of his seat, and she glanced over at him. He wouldn't be able to hold it much longer.

The tap of his fingers against the metal arm irritated her, but there was little she could do. If she complained, it might make him angry, and now wasn't the time for that. She went back to watching out for trees and waited, her breath calm and even.

She wanted Rager to be there with her, and for a moment, thought tears might fill her eyes. Every time she thought about him, she felt this warm glow in the middle of her chest, as if he knew she was thinking about him, and gave her a part of himself to reassure her. Maybe it was the tie that connected them now, but she knew he must be alright.

That gave her the strength to put up with Rex's shit and to keep the tears at bay.

She thought about the baby that grew within her, and that reminded her to be very careful however she managed to play this out. So, the news about their child hadn't exactly thrilled Rager, he'd come around, she hoped, and if not, it was too late now. It was what was expected of them, and there was nothing they could do to change those expectations.

Or the fact that she was pregnant. And so was her mom.

She hadn't thought about that for hours. What if something had happened to her mom? How far had the fighting spread? Would her parents be alright or would the aliens be super pissed and use her parents as examples? She knew Rager must be alright, but what if he wasn't and whoever took control went on a rampage.

She glared over at Rex, once again lost in his own

thoughts, his eyes closed as he tapped his fingers against the arm of his seat. This idiot had caused most of this, if not all of it. It might not be fair to blame him for it all, but she wanted to. Mainly, because she knew he'd complained from the beginning, he'd hated the fact that he wasn't allowed the same freedoms as non-shifters.

He resented it because all of his life he was the star, the schoolgirl crush and every father's hope of what a son should be. Well, misogynistic fathers, anyway. He was the golden boy, the best athlete, and even the teachers would titter when he walked by. He'd had it all, and life promised him even more before the end came. To be thrown into a bunker for years on end, then allowed out only to be made a virtual slave must have stung.

It would have stung her if that had been the position she'd been given. She could admit that and sympathize, but to be so damn selfish you put your own parents in danger to get what you wanted? That was some seriously flawed logic.

"Where are you going now?" he asked when the transporter started to veer off to the left.

"Nowhere, sorry. I'm tired and drifted for a minute." She got them back on a course that should take them in a straight line to the east, and tried to concentrate.

She hadn't lied, though, she was tired, exhausted even. She glanced down at her wrist and wished she'd worn her communicator to bed. She'd taken it off, as she always did, and now she couldn't call for help. Not that she could call with him right there, anyway. If he'd just go to sleep, she might be able to figure out how to get rid of him.

She knew he'd force her out of the transporter when she finally found somewhere to set the transporter down, and he'd probably make her sleep outside of the transporter when he finally let her rest. She could demand to be allowed the toilet and run away, maybe circle around and jump into the transporter, but would she get the glass cover closed before he got back?

She wasn't sure if the blue light the weapons used to do damage would penetrate the glass, but she didn't want to find out. That was too much like putting her life in danger.

Not something she was prepared to do. Not with her baby to think of.

She longed for some sign, some thought that would give her an idea of how to get out of this mess, but nothing came. Everything she thought about, every plan or scheme, ended with him shooting her. He might be calm right now, thinking he'd won, but she knew that the minute he thought he was about to lose he'd turn into a petulant child all over again. He'd do anything to make her suffer, and probably would when he felt like he was safe.

She wondered how much he knew about alien technology. Surely, he knew that the transporter was probably being tracked. She hoped it was anyway. Rager said they all were, but was it true? Or was it something he'd only told her? Maybe that meant the aliens knew exactly where she was and just needed to catch up to them?

If Rager had sent someone for her. He might think she was dead, or maybe he was too busy fighting off Rex's compatriots. No, she knew he'd do whatever it took to get her back. He needed her in his life, even if hadn't admitted anything of the kind to her. Besides, she was pregnant with his child. He'd want that baby back, at the very least. Right?

4

─────────

*I*f one more person asked him for guidance, he'd scream. The transporters he'd sent out to intercept Ann hadn't made contact yet, and he knew that was because Ann was still traveling. The minute it stopped, they'd scope out the scene and get back to him for further instructions.

In the meantime, he filled his hours by checking on Ann's parents, then had them and the Wolfson family sent home. They didn't know anything. The two wives had been working with an underground organization that wanted to improve the plights of the wolf shifters, but it wasn't affiliated with Rex's group in any way. They'd been fighting against them, in fact, from all the intelligence he'd received so far.

He was glad to send his mate's family back home in peace, but he wanted his own mate back, and some peace of his own. He'd been up for hours, and he wouldn't rest until she was home, but he wanted to do something about that. Instead, he was stuck running his fledgling empire. For once, he wished his brothers were there. Or his sisters. His parents. Anyone that could help him make these decisions.

It wasn't that he felt he couldn't make the right choices, he was confident about the choices he made, it was just that he didn't trust anyone else to make those right choices. His second in command should be able to, but this was too important to be left up to anyone other than an overlord. Lives depended on the decisions made now, and the future would be determined by the outcomes. He had to say he knew it, but it didn't mean he liked it.

He climbed back into his transporter and headed back toward their home. It was a mess, but most of it was salvageable. Some of it would have to be rebuilt, but it was the wings they didn't use right now, anyway. He went into the house once he'd landed and saw that the cleanup had started already. The floors were cleared, the walls washed, and debris had been removed. That must have taken an army in itself.

He didn't care, he wanted it clean and functional when Ann arrived home. Because he refused to contemplate an alternative. There was no scenario he could think of where that didn't happen. Unless Rex just killed her for the thrill of it. Which was possible, given what he knew about the man, but he hoped not. If that happened, Rex would pay in ways he couldn't imagine.

Rager thought about life on some of the exoplanets in his own galaxy and knew that he wouldn't even have to torture the man himself. There were planets that would make him beg for death. Like the one so low on breathable air that you could only last about a month before your body shut down. Every moment was like being strangled until you died in horrible pain.

That was the place he'd send the man. Whether he harmed Ann or not, he decided. That's what he deserved. A slow and agonizing death that was little more than prolonged torture. A good place for someone like Rex.

He went into their bedroom, saw the room had been untouched by the fighting and nodded. Good, she could go back to bed, as if nothing had interrupted their sleep at all. The garden had been all but destroyed by blasts, feet, and transporters, but he'd seen her cow and the horse that she loved so much, happy in the barn she'd had built for them. That was a good thing, at least. She adored her animals.

Life could almost get back to normal when he got her home, but he knew it wouldn't be the same. There was a real problem that needed to be addressed, the wolf problem, and he'd have to find a way to solve it. That was a decision for later, though. For now, he went back downstairs and found a young woman, Ann's friend Skye, in the living room.

"Have you found her yet?" the young woman asked, and Rager looked at her, his eyes narrowed.

He'd always wondered if she was a spy, but he'd never accused her of it. She was Ann's friend, a confidant probably, and Rager didn't want to take that from her, but he did have his worries about the woman.

"We know where she is, yes, but we don't have her back yet." He went and poured himself a glass of the flavored drink Ann loved so much, from a pitcher with ice on the drinks stand. He moved over to where Skye sat and refilled the glass she held, with the liquid Ann insisted was lemon-flavored tea. He didn't really care for it, but it was something to drink.

"How long will that take, to get her back, I mean?" The woman was brave, and she met Rager's orange gaze steadily, without flinching. He had to respect her for that.

"I don't know. It depends on how long they stay in the transporter. We can't get to them if they stay inside it, the vehicle is impenetrable. If he takes her out of it, however, we can get to him."

"That little prick. I knew I should have choked him when I had the chance." Rager heard her mutter and looked at her more closely, his eyes narrowed in a frown.

"When you had the chance?"

"Yeah, he, um, he comes to the bar, at the edge of the sector, that I go to sometimes. Causes trouble all the time, and got in my face one night." She didn't volunteer anything more than that and Rager decided he needed to know more.

"You were in a bar on your own?" He looked her over, saw a powerful woman, with very little fat, and a look about her that said she was capable of taking care of herself.

"I'm not the typical woman you'll find in one of your wife's little luncheons , Rager. I'm not into men, if you get my drift." She said it with a waggle of her eyebrows and a tone in her voice that probably should have meant something.

"You aren't into men?" It was a phrase that mystified him. He'd learned most of the American phraseology, but this one stumped him.

"I prefer women when it comes to romantic relationships."

"Ah! Right, I get it." He nodded his head, a memory flashed in his mind. "Ann told me that, but, forgive me, it slipped my mind."

"No problem, you're under a lot of stress. Is there anything I can do to help?" She seemed genuinely concerned about her friend, but he couldn't think of anything she could possibly do in the situation.

"I don't think so. You're welcome to wait if you'd like, but I really don't know how long it will take." Rager looked around for the man that served as a butler here but didn't see him. Perhaps he'd been killed? That would be a shame, he'd come to like the stuffy man with the cold attitude and overbearing manner. "How did you get in?"

"The soldier at the door let me in." She pointed at the door, as if to explain, and he nodded.

"Right. Forgot about that too."

"Have you eaten? You should probably eat something. It will help you focus," she advised, and he shook his head.

"No, but you could be right. Care to try Ann's ideas of vegetarian food?" He gestured her to follow him, and he went back to the kitchen. He found some leftover zucchini casserole and put it in a pan to reheat on the stove. Skye had tasted the casserole before and said she'd join him.

They sat at the kitchen table, and he had to admit, it was weird. He should be out looking for Ann, instead, he was here, waiting on more demands for answers. Waiting on information. Waiting on her to be safe. Just... waiting.

He took a bite of the casserole and washed it down

with the strangely flavored tea. He wanted to rush out of the kitchen, beat his fist into a wall, and roar his way across the sky until he found his mate, but instead, he took another bite of food and wondered at this particular custom.

Even in his own world, food was used as a distraction, a way to comfort, and as part of celebrations. It was the same here, though they were still finding creative ways to use canned and dried foods as they waited for fresh produce and meat to become available on a larger scale. People found food important though, and many of the homes that were now occupied had a garden with fruit trees and bushes.

The work of his people had helped to speed up the process of growing trees and plants, even animals in some cases, so that his people and any survivors found would be able to eat a proper diet. But it was also so that his people and the people of Earth could join in celebrating new life with food as an ice-breaker.

"I'm going to head back down to the clinic, I just wanted to come by to ask about Ann," Skye said as she finished and stood up from the table. "I hope you'll let me know when she returns home? She is my friend, after all."

"I'll make sure she calls you herself. After she's rested, and able to, of course."

"Indeed. Thank you, sir." She tilted her head for a moment and left.

If she was working down at the clinic, she'd need to rush back to check on the many patients there. From what Rager had been told, the place was overflowing with wounded humans, caught in the crossfire, and likely hiding a revolutionary or two. Not that the clinic was to blame if there were fugitives hiding with the wounded. It was just that they would be removed and taken to the ship for care before they were questioned, and a sentence given.

Rager still wasn't sure what to do with them, but it was a question he decided to talk about with Ann when she came home. She loved to talk with him about the plans for her planet, and she was an intelligent woman. She was also a pseudo-ambassador for her people. They could discuss ideas together and it helped him to get a better picture of what the results might be.

It was an unexpected benefit to having a mate, and one he was grateful for. So many of his people had abrasive, simpering wives that wanted to ingratiate themselves to him. They couldn't think beyond the next week, much less the next month or year. Or even decades from now. Rager needed to think well beyond the here and now, which was why he remained in his chair.

His connection to his mate allowed him the knowledge that she was safe, but not a lot more. For now, he'd have to take that knowledge as all he would get. Boot-steps rang out from the front door and Rager turned, a look of concern on his face.

He saw a messenger, one of the smaller of his kind, but still more powerful than any of the best human specimens about. "Sir, you're needed."

"Of course, I am, Milkos, let's get back to the ship." He followed the man out of the house and before he could think about it too hard, he was back on the ship.

He gave new orders, kept old orders in place in some situations, and looked over the reports from some of his generals below. "The fighting is almost over?"

"Yes, sir." A general, a man named Denlux, snapped to attention and answered Rager. Rager noted the mint green eyes showed signs of fatigue and found it petty, but couldn't but feel glad that he wasn't the only one.

"Good. We all need our beds." Rager flipped through a file with pictures, maps, and detailed accounts of the information gained when each new fighting group surrendered or, well, died.

"The last group is camped out on a hill, but we're about to take them out with a transporter if they don't surrender." The general shook his head in confusion. "I still don't understand what this fight is about. I don't think I'll ever understand these earthlings."

"It's not hard to understand really. These aren't

humans alone. They're shifter people too. They're more like us than we care to admit." Rager let slip a truth that nobody had spoken about.

While his people took on the characteristics of humans, their DNA wasn't pure. Some of it was the cause of the wolf shifters below. The DNA they'd left behind had come to life when the cataclysm released certain chemicals that had been trapped in the Earth's crust so that the mostly humans with alien DNA had manifested as wolf shifters.

It wasn't something they spoke about often, not even among themselves.

"I suppose you're right, Overlord," the man said and sagged a little.

Rager looked at him sharply. He supposed Rager was right? At any other time, he'd upbraid the man for his insolence, but he was too tired to remind the man that even when he was tired, he should be careful of how he worded things.

Besides, his ego wasn't that fragile, he decided.

"Good," he said and snapped the file shut. "Let's start getting the soldiers in bed in shifts, keep guards posted and lookouts ready. Keep the scanners running up here to check for violence as well. And let me know if there's any news about the fires that are still burning."

Some of the fights had caused fires to break out in some of the abandoned buildings in a sector that was normally empty. There were still resources there that could be used, and buildings that could have been refurbished. He wanted the fires out to protect what was left. The thought of the fires spreading to populated areas was not a good one either, so the crews were down there trying to get some of those out.

It had been a long night, he thought, and he looked out to see that the horizon had started to turn light already. It wasn't bright, just a faint difference in the horizon, but he knew it wouldn't be long before the sun was up. Hopefully, his mate would be home soon, and they could sleep the day away. He probably shouldn't take any time with her, after he'd assured himself she was cared for and given medical care if she needed it. He should probably get right back to work. Make sure the uprising was finished and everyone put in their proper place and leave her to sleep off her ordeal.

Fuck that.

5

"That's it, Ann. I can't take it anymore. Set this thing down on the nearest thing that looks like ground and let me out." Rex snapped up out of his seat and glared down at her, his face red with anger and with what she was certain must be petulance.

He looked like a child she used to babysit, that would wake up from his nap too early sometimes. He was always cranky then, that little child, and red in the face, ready to do a ton of whining. She would feel pity for Rex, but there was an alternative to the amount of time he'd had to hold off his body's needs. He could have used the device on the transporter, but he was too good for that.

There was another thing that made her conscience twinge, but not too much. She hadn't told him the lava, water, and rocky mountain tops were gone now, and she'd made him wait for as long as possible by doing that. She cast another glance at him before she looked down at the ground again to find somewhere that wouldn't put them in danger.

This could be her chance, she thought and tried to keep her face calm. He was desperate to relieve his bladder now, and she hoped it would make him clumsy. She saw an open field below, clear of everything but grass and a few trees at the edges. She put the transporter down in the middle of the field and turned to get up.

He was already out of his seat, and by the section where the stairs would go down so he could get to the ground. When he heard her stand up, he turned and held his hand out to her, his face a snarl of anger. The Rex she knew and detested was back, that quickly.

"No, you stay right there. I don't want you out there trying to run away. Stay there and don't you dare move!" He picked up the alien weapon he'd brought along with him and headed out of the transporter. She watched him run toward the trees, her breath held. Was he really that stupid? No, surely, he wasn't.

It would be so easy if he really did plan to leave her in the transporter. Her lungs started to feel as if they'd swelled in her chest and she took in a soft breath. She was too stunned to believe it for a few seconds, and she just stood there, in front of her seat, and waited for it all to make sense.

She watched as he dodged behind a tree and fumbled with the front of his pants. He was a good 350 feet away. She gaped at him now, her brain raced over how stupid he was. She'd known, she'd known for a long time that he was arrogant, but this? This went well past stupid and maybe straight into moronic.

Did she have time? She glanced at Rex, his head tilted back now, completely relaxed, as he relieved himself. What made him so stupid, she wondered, did he think she was glad he'd kidnapped her? Or did he not care and think he had her cowed?

With a raised left eyebrow and lips pursed in a smirk, Ann closed the transporter glass shell, every breath shallow as she waited for the glass to finally close.

"Come on, come on, close," she muttered softly as the stairs lifted into the transporter and the glass came down. Each second was a second he might notice that she was about to flee, and she wanted to be protected when he did finally notice. She didn't want a stray beam from the alien gun to blast through and hit her.

She kept her finger on the button to lower the shell, her heart pounding way too fast as the seconds ticked by. Slowly, it lowered, was it always that slow or was that something new? Was fate against her?

"Please, please close!" she begged the protective shell

and watched as the gap slowly started to get smaller. She glanced back and forth, between that gap and Rex, her face scrunched into a grimace, as the glass edged closer to the closed point.

The shell finally settled into the groove that ran around the perimeter of the transporter and Ann started to lift the machine. She wanted to whoop in delight, she wanted to give him the finger as she lifted off, but she also wanted to get away from him. Right now, that was more important than anything else.

She saw Rex turn, his mouth hung open in shock, as she began to rise. Apparently, it hadn't occurred to him that this was exactly what would happen if he left her alone in the transporter. What an idiot.

She could see he was down there shouting and gesticulating, but she didn't care about that. All she cared about was how quickly his face disappeared as she escaped. There was nothing he could do about it from down there but scream and rant in the field. She was no longer his prisoner. Relief wanted to flood into her veins, but she clamped down on it, determined not to mess this up.

She started to pull the machine back away from him as it lifted higher into the sky, just in case. She didn't want to be directly over him, where he could hit her, if he fired that weapon.

As if he'd heard her thought, Rex lifted the weapon

and fired it. Ann flinched away and turned to face the other side of the transporter. She waited for an explosion, anything, but nothing happened. She turned back to see that the blue light just bounced off the transporter and didn't make the slightest sound as it did so.

Ann laughed, a real laugh of amusement, and stood up to look down at Rex below. Slowly, with a grin of triumph, she held her free hand up and waved as she turned the transporter to head back towards California. It wasn't a friendly wave, it was definitely a 'haha, fucker, I escaped' kind of wave, and she laughed again as she sat back down.

She hadn't had a lot of time to think when he'd left her in the transporter, and she didn't really think about too much now, she just took tiny little breaths and pushed the transporter further away from Rex. Away from the danger he'd threatened her with.

When the field was gone, and the ragged peaks of mountains came into view, she started to relax. Until that point, she'd been afraid that the engine would fail, or some kind of geyser would open up from the ground below and knock her out of the sky. Anything could have happened to mess up her escape, and she was well aware of it. Life wasn't always easy, and just when you thought you were good, life had a way of laughing at you like a high school bully that's just seen you fall flat on your face into a pile of dog poo.

She swallowed when she saw the first glow of the lava fields, took a deep breath, and lifted the transporter higher. The transporter kept the temperature inside at a comfortable level, if slightly cool, so she didn't feel the heat, but she could see the glow of the unimaginable hell below. She was kind of glad she'd left Rex on the other side of that mess. He'd have to walk a long way to get around that huge rift in the earth's crust. Maybe further than a person could walk.

He could always fly across it, maybe, but he definitely wouldn't be back in her part of the world anytime soon. Not unless Rager sent someone after him to deal with him properly. She didn't know what her mate would do once she got back, and right now, she didn't care.

She was safe and free of him, at last!

That's when it occurred to her that she might have just sentenced him to death. Her hand on the joystick pulled back a little. Maybe she shouldn't leave him out there in the wild like that? She should go back for him, right?

After all, deep down in there somewhere, he was still the boy that had taken her breath away for all of those years. They'd survived the cataclysm together, and then been stuck in a bunker for years together. Was it right for her to just… leave him? Would her parents forgive her? Would his?

Ann felt a twinge of guilt and something that might be regret. The transporter slowed its progress, but it didn't stop. Her head turned, and she looked back, in the direction of where she'd left Rex, only an hour ago. Maybe she should go back and at least drop some food down to him. She had plenty in the cupboards on board the transporter.

She was just about to turn around, to head back to help him out, for old time's sake, for Amanda, his mother's sake, when her jaw went tight and she took a deep breath. No. She couldn't offer someone like him help. She thought about the explosions that had woken her up, the people that had probably died, because of him, and the guilt melted away.

His words replayed in her mind, about how he was going to kill her baby, about how she was scum, and she remembered the way he'd treated her, especially after she'd been mated to Rager. Her hand pushed the transporter forward again. He'd just have to learn to survive or die out here. Maybe, if he was lucky, Rager would send someone out to take him to a prison somewhere far away. She didn't know and she didn't care.

Her heart hardened to him completely, after so many years of hope, adoration, and blindness to his faults. He'd been her first crush, the first man she thought she loved. But he hadn't been. That was Rager. It might not make any sense, but she did love the alien that was her mate, she loved him more than she could have thought possible. And she needed to be in his arms, safe, locked away from the world. Whether it made sense or not, she didn't care.

Exhaustion ate at her exhilaration, and even though she wanted to watch every mile that passed, she knew she'd have to sleep soon. She set the autopilot on a course to return her to the house and pushed the seat Rex had stretched out in into a flat surface, almost like a narrow bed. She used the facilities, had a long drink of water from a glass jar, and had one of the small snacks she kept in the transporter's food area.

She wished she had her watch communicator again. She'd call Rager and her parents, tell them she was on her way back home, but she didn't have it. The transporter might have some kind of communication device, but she hadn't figured out where it was, if one existed. With a push against a panel, she found a thin blanket and a pillow, and put them on the chair. With a grateful sigh, she dimmed the lights and sank down onto the chair.

She was so tired, she thought she'd drop off right to sleep. Her mind whirled around, focused, and then span off again on some new line of thought instead. Was the house the right place to go back to? Had the sector been destroyed? How far had the fighting spread? What would be the repercussions?

It was all a tangle of thoughts that she tried to tease out, to settle her mind so that she could sleep. There was a low hum, not really a noise, almost like road noise, that came from the transporter, and the sound soothed her. Her thoughts started to slow, at last, and it wasn't so hard to concentrate on one thing.

Rager. He was safe. She could feel it. When she got home, she wanted to tell him how she felt, that she loved him, but he wasn't the kind of guy that whispered I love you into your ears now, was he, she thought to herself. He was an "I'll fuck you 'til your legs turn to jelly" kind of guy, definitely, and she loved that, but she wanted to hear those three little words, too.

Maybe she shouldn't be so greedy, but she couldn't help it. From the odd orange glow of his eyes to the tips of his toes, so far below his head she had to crane her neck to look up at him, she loved every square inch of her man. His tattooed skin was art she loved to trace, his skin was silky smooth and covered the hard planes of his muscles. His body, oh man, his body was art too. Everything about him made her melt, but it wasn't all lust. She loved those parts of him, but most of all she loved his brain, the way he wanted to do everything right, the way he wanted to create this new world, and how intelligent he was about it all.

Sometimes, he'd argue, or growl that she didn't understand, but he'd think about whatever it was, and usually come back and say she was right. That meant he was a good listener, and he valued her opinion. But was it love?

She pulled the red blanket beneath her chin and stared out through the glass of the roof. The sky was still dark, but there was a glow, the warning that dawn was on the way.

Did her mate love her?

Did it matter?

In the end, she supposed it didn't matter, she was mated to him for life, whether they loved each other or not. He'd said once that their bond went beyond love, that it was deeper than just that physical and mental connection. How could that be, she'd wondered, but now, as she felt a warm glow in her chest, she understood. But was it love?

"You're never happy, are you, Ann?" she said out loud and turned over in the chair. She stuck her hand under the pillow and wiggled her head around until it was just right.

Shouldn't the father of her child love her? She let her free hand roam until she found the spot where she thought the baby was. She cupped that spot and smiled. Her baby. Her child.

She'd have someone to give all of her love to if Rager didn't want it, she knew. Still, he would have her love, if he wanted it or not. She wouldn't stop loving him, just because he didn't say it back to her.

She started to drift, her thoughts almost on pause between each breath she took. She wanted to sleep, she wanted to think, until finally, there was nothing but peace.

6

*R*ager watched as the sun came up over the horizon. He was in his office, wrecked but ready for battle if it was necessary. He was a soldier after all. He hadn't earned the top position on this mission just because of who his parents were. He'd earned the right to be king here.

He'd spent years in battle as his people fought to maintain control of their world. There'd been battles with alien races, races that wanted to subjugate his people, throughout their history. They had always overcome those threats.

The people of his world began to populate other planets over time, a grand experiment to spread their genes and to discover new worlds. His people wanted knowledge above all things and contemplated complex problems to gain that knowledge. They'd accomplished things other races had only dreamed about.

Even the people here had contemplated time travel, but they'd been too focused on war with each other to accomplish it. They would head in the right direction for a short time, they would discover something new to them, but then they would look at the wrong application of that new knowledge. They would use it to destroy rather than to explore.

It was a shame really, and one of the reasons his people had left them to destroy themselves. There was hope that the ones that had survived their own stupidity would be able to learn that life was not meant to be war and poverty, subjugation and destruction. He'd hoped to teach them a new way.

He could see now that the people would need a lot more education than he'd planned to implement. With a sigh, he ran his hand across his face, stuck his booted feet up on his desk, and leaned back in his chair. The sun penetrated his eyelids, made the burning orbs ache, so he put his hands over them.

She'll be back soon, he told himself.

His brain throbbed against his skull, a warning that he needed sleep, but he wouldn't be able to relax, not until Ann was back. A rumble filled the air as he pictured her, safe in his arms, their bare skin against each other, her head on his chest. She was so trusting, so gentle, but so fierce too. He knew she'd been terrified of him, but she'd faced him bravely. And she'd given in to their true mating without a fight.

She could have fought it, denied that he was her one-true-mate, but she was sensible too. She'd wanted him as much as he wanted her.

And she'd given herself up to him. That didn't mean she allowed him to walk all over her though. She'd found ways to get him to come around to her way of thinking, or pushed him into providing her with items or information only he could give.

Now, she would be the mother of his child. She'd faced that just as bravely as she did anything else. He was proud of her, proud of the way she faced her problems. It was more than he'd been able to do when she'd revealed her pregnancy.

He regretted his lukewarm response now. He'd thought about it quite a few times throughout the hours that passed. He hadn't wanted a child so quickly, but it was on the way. He wondered now if it was a girl or a boy.

Would it look like her, gentle and breath-taking, or would it look like him? Fierce, harsh some might say, but definitely a warrior. An overlord.

His child, this first child, would be the overlord

when his days were done. If it lived, of course. He had brought the technology the new world would need to ensure survival rates were good with each new child that was born. Things happened though, and the alien technology could perform miracles in many cases, but sometimes, accidents happened that did damage too quickly.

He had to stop thinking so far ahead, he reminded himself. Sometimes, you need to focus on the present, be in that moment, and make quick decisions. So far, he had done that for most of the night. Now, he had to make another.

When Ann's transporter landed, he'd be notified. He'd have to make a decision. Should his soldiers rush the vehicle and occupants, or wait?

He tapped the fingers of his left hand against the armrest and tried to decide. Take that chance or let it go? It was a risk.

He wanted to be out there, to be close to her, but he knew the minute he left he'd be called back to deal with something. He'd had thirty minutes of peace so far, he knew it wouldn't last much longer.

He put on some of the music he'd discovered through his mate and was surprised to find that his foot still had the energy to tap in time with the rhythm of a song by a man with a very strange name, singing about needing some flowers and a time machine. He had a feeling that would be a good idea. He could go back in time, make his reaction to Ann's news about the baby a better one, and make her smile.

But going back in time could be a slippery slope that leads to madness. His people knew that well. His people could fold space, and in a way time, but it was more about space. Time was a concept anyway, it wasn't real, but that was a whole other mess of thoughts he was too tired to think about right now.

He sat up, tried to rub the throb out of his temples, and waited.

He didn't have to wait long. Someone soon knocked at his door and he called out to tell them to come in.

"Sir, your mate's transporter has changed course. It sat down for a little while, but now it's coming back. From what we can tell, it's locked in to come back here to the house." A female soldier, a woman he thought was named Drinda, came in and stood at attention as she relayed her news.

Relief sapped all of his strength for a moment. She was on her way back. He hoped.

"Good. Bring in a contingent of soldiers, place them around the house. Just in case."

"Yes, sir." The woman hesitated, and then she spoke again. She was a pretty woman, with light brown hair and yellow eyes that managed to be quite lovely rather than odd. His people all had odd eye colors, though, so it wasn't unusual to him. "Your mate, sir, she isn't responding to our calls."

"Perhaps the traitorous rat that took her is still with her." He brushed off the news, but as she left, he had to wonder. She hadn't used her watch communicator either.

The hours passed, the sun rose, and he finally had a nap for an hour. He used the downstairs bathroom to shower and changed in the bedroom but didn't stay in there long. He went back downstairs and was immediately met with a living room full of patiently waiting people. He'd planned to have some lunch and then get back to the ship, but these people couldn't wait.

He reminded himself to give the butler orders not to let anyone but Ann in after he dealt with this bunch. The problem was, people kept coming in.

"We need permission to open a building for some newcomers that arrived, sir." A studious looking man, short, bald, and round with glasses that had been glued together far too many times asked, with a clipboard in his hands. Somewhere he'd found a rather threadbare suit, an atrocious olive green threaded with yellow, and it served to make him look even more studious somehow.

"You have it." Rager waved the man away, and a woman rushed up.

Dressed in a long, flowing black skirt and a white t-shirt with long sleeves, she had the voice of a mouse and the bearing of one as well.

"Sir, we need to know if we can open a house of prayer." She backed away when he rolled his eyes and growled. "I'm sorry."

"If you feel you must, then you may. But don't cause problems or that permission will be rescinded." Rager couldn't imagine the woman would ever get the gumption to cause problems, but she was in front of him, in his home, so maybe he was wrong. He'd have to have his soldiers watch her and her group.

People could have religion if they wanted to, but it wasn't a part of his people's lives. They didn't need it, and as far as he could see, man had used religion to fight wars and subjugate people for thousands of years on this planet. That wouldn't be the case with this incarnation of life on this planet.

He went on to settle a dispute between two mayors of the villages that made up the districts of this sector. One man wanted to use a small strip of land between their two homes to build onto his house. The other refused to allow it.

"Do you have any children?" Rager asked simply, and the man that wanted to build huffed up his chest. He must be in his sixties, so he should have been wise enough to know why this was a bad idea.

"No, Overlord, but that doesn't mean..." but Rager cut him off.

"It goes. John here has children and one on the way. If he can cope with the room he has, so can you. Otherwise, we can remove you from your post and find you a larger property somewhere else. Perhaps outside of the sector would be more suitable for you?" The man, dressed in a luxurious suit he must have scoured the sector for, shrank into himself and lost a lot of his huff as Rager spoke.

"No, you're right, Overlord. I beg your pardon."

Rager sat on the edge of a couch and watched the men go. A woman came in, heavily pregnant, and with two small children behind her. He frowned. Why was this woman so desperate looking? She and her children were all clean and tidy, but their clothes were threadbare and patched in places.

"What can I do for you?" Rager asked pleasantly and looked at the children that hid behind their mother. She had on ragged jeans and a thin flannel shirt stretched over her big belly. The shirt had been covered in patches, and he was certain the pleats were actually tearing that she'd repaired.

"I, well, sir, I've been trying not to ask, because I know

you're busy, but I need to change the village I live in. The man there, he's not very nice, and he's kicked my children and me out of our home to turn it into a parking spot for his transporter." She looked desperate, her brown eyes were hollow and bruised, her face thin, with a long bruise that ran down her face and down somewhere below her shirt.

Rager scowled and looked at the children. They were nearly in tears, hidden behind their mother's thin legs. "Give me that man's name, and please take the house four doors down from mine. It's a little bit of a walk so I'll have one of my people take you."

For a moment there was a flurry of activity as Rager got the man's name, ordered his men to remove him from power and take him to a holding area for investigation. If the woman's allegations were true, he'd be removed from power and kicked out of the sector. Rager also ordered his people to find whatever the woman needed, to bring her food, and to take her to get clothes for her and the children.

"Thank you, Overlord. I can't thank you enough." She looked as if she wanted to hug him, but held herself back.

"It's my duty, Nancy. There's also a clinic in our sector for pregnant women. I'll get you the address for that."

She couldn't stop smiling, and Rager could see that

once she'd been fed and had some rest, she'd be a very beautiful woman.

"Do you have a mate?" He wasn't sure she'd be quite ready for one, not if she'd lost a man, but he'd find out if she wanted one.

"No, Overlord, he was killed a few months ago, before you came. An accident in our bunker." Her eyes teared up, but she lifted her head and looked him in the eye when she spoke.

"Alright. Do you want one?" He asked it bluntly, as a show of respect. If he knew the answer now, it would save a lot of problems later.

"I haven't thought about it, really. I wasn't offered one in my village, but then, I think the mayor had, ahem, plans." Her eyes glanced over her children to indicate that it wasn't a talk for now. Later, without the young ones present would be better.

"I understand. Please talk to my people, let them know what they need to know and tell them what you need. We'll deal with this man."

She nodded her head and a female soldier came to lead her away. The house he'd placed her in was a smaller mansion than his, but it would give her and the children the room they would need. If she could deal with that much space.

Even Ann had remarked on how different it was to be above ground. Sometimes, she'd told him, she missed being underground. Many of the people that came to him also said the same thing. Many had less room than Ann and her group lived in and found it difficult to be out in the open, and large houses bothered them. A few had even gone back to live in their bunkers, away from everyone.

Rager could understand them all, once you became used to something, it was hard to change.

"Sir, the transporter is here!"

Rager froze. Ann was back!

He was worried, very worried, because she hadn't communicated at all, and as he left the room to head outside, dread filled him. When the soldiers outside reported they hadn't seen anyone inside, his heart went cold and he was certain it had stopped. He stood still as a pain unlike anything he'd ever felt before coursed through him.

But he could feel her, he thought. He could still feel her in his soul, so she had to be alright. Perhaps the transporter was empty?

He rushed to the transporter and placed his palm in the scanner. It was only his or her touch that would open the transporter, so he had to be the one that went in. Nobody could do it for him. Not that he'd have anybody else do it. This was his job.

He watched the stairs come down, his heart a dull thud in his chest as he closed his eyes.

"She's there, sir," a voice behind him said.

Rager opened his eyes and saw his mate, asleep in the passenger chair, her hand tucked under her chin. He leaned into the frame where the stairs came down and took in a deep breath of relief. He wouldn't have to kill anyone, not yet anyway. She was safe, at last.

7

"I'm fine, Skye, please stop fussing over me." Ann brushed her friend's hands away and sat back on the examination table.

"It wasn't that long ago that you were kidnapped, Ann. We need to check everything."

"It was months ago, Skye!" Ann's hands went to her stomach, much rounder than it had been that day.

A day she didn't like to talk about with anyone. Especially Amanda, the mother of the man that had caused them all so many problems.

"That might be, but the stress is still there. That's why you won't talk about it."

"More like…" but she didn't finish. She couldn't say the word that she thought about so very much.

Guilt.

She couldn't help it, she felt bad that she'd left Rex

out there in the wild. Rager's soldiers had scoured the place for the man but had found no signs of him anywhere. Every time she saw his mother or his father, that guilt only increased. Both of them had told her she'd done what was best, the only thing she could have done. She'd made sure she escaped from him.

They might not blame her, but the sadness in Amanda's eyes didn't make her feel better at all. She had nightmares now, about the things that might have happened to him. Amanda's heart was broken, however, and Ann felt like some of that was her fault.

"Look, I know what happened was his fault, but I chose to leave him out there. I chose to let him die… maybe." She'd said it, at last, and hopefully, that would shut Skye up.

"You're going to have to find a better way to cope with this, Ann. It's not good for you or the baby. I know that's an unkind thing to say, that you need to just deal with it, but it's true. Sometimes, that's all you can do. Deal with it and get on with your life."

Skye turned away but Ann still caught a look on Skye's lovely face that made her wonder. What had Skye had to deal with?

"You're one to talk." Ann pushed her long white shirt back down and sat up on the table. "You have your own troubles."

"I'm not carrying a baby." Skye made a face at her

and then spoiled it all by laughing. "But yeah, I guess we all have our burdens to bear. This one, however, shouldn't be one you bear alone."

"Whatever." Ann waved her hand and laughed at the childishness of her comment. "Fine."

"How are you otherwise? I know you've had time to adjust, to get back into the swing of things…" her words trailed off.

"Everything is fine, really. I just, I can't go to Mom's often. I can't face Amanda anymore, you know?" Ann turned and picked up the bag that Katy, the super-stalker chihuahua since she had got home, had nestled down in. Ann hadn't even known the small dog was there until she got into the clinic and Katy yipped to go outside to potty.

"I understand, I do." Skye put a hand on her shoulder, and Ann walked into her arms. The two hugged before Ann stepped away.

"I just don't know how to get over it, Skye. How do I deal with it? I left a man out in the world without food or water. He didn't even have matches."

"I didn't know Rex well, but he's a conniving bastard. I guarantee you, he's out there wrapped in a bearskin, roasting some poor bunny rabbit on a spit over a fire. He's not dead. He's too damn mean to die."

Ann had to laugh at the picture Skye drew for her with words and rolled her eyes at her own stupidity.

"You're probably right, you know. He is too mean to just wither away and die."

"He'll be like that guy from that old TV show, the one about zombies that everybody used to love? The bad guy that always managed to survive?"

"I remember that. We just have to make sure we're not stupid enough to let him back into our world. That was their problem. Always letting in people that would cause problems."

"Speaking of…" Skye looked at her, a delicately arched eyebrow crooked.

"I don't know if there are more people yet, or not. They're screening them all now before they let them in. No matter how many have to wait in holding areas." She had barely seen Rager the last few days because of it.

"I'm just glad he's so paranoid about Rex getting back here somehow. I'm not sure I like being chipped." Skye paused to rub at a spot on the bottom of her wrist before she continued. "It does make it easier to prove who we are, though."

Ann rubbed at the spot where her own chip was and nodded in agreement. "I didn't like it either, but I'm with you. It has its merits."

"And what about that woman, Nancy?" Skye sat down in a simple office chair of black metal and black plastic to look up at Ann.

"She's in her own home now, not far from us. Turns

out that place was turning into a hellhole. It's on the edge of our sector, so there weren't a lot of patrols out there. The man has been sent off-planet." Ann let her eyes go wide and Skye's eyebrow lifted again.

"That bad, was he?"

"Yep, I won't go into it, but let's say it's good he kicked her out. It beat the alternative." They both knew that being sent off-planet was a punishment that was saved for those the aliens deemed beyond redemption. Rager had explained the man's crimes to her, but she didn't want to think about them.

"Damn. That poor woman."

"Women!" Ann interrupted, and Skye's blue eyes narrowed.

"What do you mean?"

"He seems to have fathered a few children. They're coming here so that the aliens can, well, they have to decide whether they want to terminate the pregnancies or not."

"Fucking hell!" Skye blinked with surprise. "They'll allow that?"

"In some cases, ones like this." Ann breathed a sigh of pity for the women. "It's terrible for them, and it's their choice."

"It is." Skye stood up to hug her friend again. "It's not all fun and games being mated to the Overlord, is it?"

"Not all the time. But sometimes, oh man. You don't

know what you're missing." Ann didn't want to wallow in sorrow, guilt, or pity anymore. As Skye had said, it wasn't good for the baby. She pulled back to wink at her friend, slid her shoes into the simple leather boots she'd worn in, and wiggled her toes in her socks. "Sometimes it's pure heaven."

"I don't want to know. Eww! It's like hearing your parents."

"Stop! Yuck, Skye! It's bad enough Mom's proving they still do it without you talking about it!" Ann held her hands up over her ears in mock horror and walked out of the exam room.

"She's due soon, your poor mom. Twins at her age. She's brave." Skye's smile said she really did respect Ann's mom.

"She's doing her part. But I think she's scared. And excited. Same as me. Excited to see how our children turn out but scared to raise them in this new world. They won't know our old lives at all."

"No, it's a shame really. But, I guess we can find some movies, somewhere. And we are finding more things every day. We have the books, our memories. We'll find a way to show them who we were, what we should work to avoid being in the future." Skye looked around the empty waiting area and then back at Ann.

"I guess they're all things we're going to have to deal with as we go along, aren't they?" Ann leaned against the wall and cradled her stomach. It wasn't large, not yet, but it was getting there. It was enough to make her back curve and put pressure on places she'd never actually felt before.

"You going home now? I can make us some lunch," Skye offered, but Ann shook her head.

"No, I'm going to see Rager. He's coming home for lunch to find out what you've revealed today." Ann widened her eyes for effect.

"It was just a checkup. He doesn't need to worry, you're fine."

"I know, and he does, but he's been… protective, I guess, since I came home." She smiled, a secret smile of a woman pleased with her man. "It's nice, really. He comes home more, and he makes sure he asks about the baby."

But he still hadn't come to an appointment with her.

That dimmed her smile a bit, but not much. He was a busy man. He'd be home waiting for her, that was enough.

She told her friend goodbye and left to head home. She drove straight home, eager to see her man. He'd been a lot more protective since she came home, but he'd also been more eager to have her. In bed, over the back of the couch in the living room, in the bathtub, wherever the mood struck him, he'd turn that smile on that made her melt and she'd start to take her clothes off.

Sometimes he even let her get them all off before he had his head between her legs.

She giggled as she put the transporter down and walked into the house. When she got in, she could hear Rager talking to someone. A quick glance told her it was a meeting, so she went to the kitchen. She let them know she was home, then went up to their bedroom and out to the veranda. It was still her favorite place in the house.

It had taken some time, but the house was back to normal, and everything had been peaceful. The leaders of the revolution had been banished from the alien sectors, forever, and had chips between their shoulder blades, where they wouldn't be easily removed. To ensure they didn't get help removing the chips, each person was left in a different location, far from anyone else. This would also make it hard for them to get back to the sectors.

Lunch was brought up, but Rager didn't appear, so she ate on her own with Katy curled up in her lap. It was the life she'd become used to, and instead of complaining, she put her music on and pulled out a cloth bag from her closet. Back out on the veranda, she took out the projects she'd been working on.

Her mom's babies would be here soon, and it was cool already, so she'd taken apart several old sweaters she'd found and cleaned the yarn to make blankets and outfits for the babies. She'd even found some yarn that had managed to survive the apocalypse in sealed plastic, but they weren't the best colors for boys .

Her mom was having a boy and a girl so the girl colors would be fine for that baby . She hadn't found out what she was having yet. The baby was always in the wrong position when they did a scan, so it was still a mystery.

She'd already made two afghans with crochet patterns she'd found in a book in the library, with instructions on how to do it, and she wanted to try her hand at knitting. She had to finish the outfits first, though. She'd knit two more blankets or so, then try to make some socks and other things.

The legs didn't exactly match on one outfit, so she spent the rest of the afternoon sorting that, and then started to try to follow the instructions for knitting. Rager found her there, an hour later, in tears at the mess that she'd made.

"Ann! Why are you crying?" He knelt down in front of his mate. She had on a long sweater now over her t-shirt and a pair of leggings, and he brushed the panels of the warm garment away to cradle her stomach.

"I can't figure out how to do this knitting shit!" she exclaimed through her tears. She looked down at him, miserable at her inability to master something that was supposed to be so simple.

"Have you ever done it before?" he asked patiently as he wiped at her tears with his large thumbs.

"No," she whispered through a tight throat.

"Have you ever seen it actually done before?" His voice was patient and he leaned in to kiss her damp cheek. His orange eyes met hers and her heart swelled with the understanding and… maybe it was love that she could see. Her lips crooked up at the corners.

"No." She looked miserable and she knew it, but she couldn't help it. She'd looped, twisted, poked, and pulled it all apart, time after time, but she couldn't seem to make what she did match with what was in the handy-dandy instructional picture.

"I'll find out if any of the people in our sector know and have them come to teach you if they want to. How does that sound?" He was still patient as he knelt there, his face wreathed in an understanding smile.

"That sounds good." She pushed the tangled yarn away and put her hands over his as they went back to her belly. "I can feel it moving now. It kicks a lot too, especially today."

"How far are you now?" he asked, and she had to think about it.

"I think around six months." She thought about it and spoke again. "That's what Skye figured anyway."

"We have to figure out a better way of keeping track of dates." He sat down on the floor, at her feet, and kicked his legs out. We could always start a new calendar."

"I think the humans on this side of Earth are used to our calendar. A new one might be confusing." She thought it might be too hard to learn a new one, no matter how simple it might be.

"You're right. Even if it wasn't exactly accurate." His smile made her grin and nudge at his legs with her feet.

"Well, that's as may be, but it doesn't change the fact that it's the one we know." She moved from the chair and straddled him with her legs. "Besides, your mate says she doesn't want to learn a whole new calendar. She likes the old one."

She hovered over him, a grin on her face as he leaned back to look up at her, hunger already in his fiery eyes. His smell filled her nose, and her own desire flared into life. She moved closer, her lips almost on his eyes. She flicked her eyes up to his and gave him a sultry smile.

"We'll keep your calendar then. Just kiss me, Ann, before I go insane."

So, she did.

8

"The baby is fine, Ann, and if you want to know what you're having, I can tell you now."

Ann looked over at Rager, and he smiled down at her. It was the first time he'd come in with her, and like a miracle, their baby had finally let them know what gender it was.

"I think," but her words trailed off as a long scream came from the hall followed by a volley of profanity.

"Help, my wife's in labor!" a man screamed from the waiting area, and everyone but Ann ran into the room.

It must be earthlings, Ann thought, the man had said wife.

"I'll tie your fucking dick in a knot, you fucking animal!" Ann heard a woman, obviously in deep pain, growl. "Come near me again, think I'm ever going through this again, and see what you get!"

Ann's jaw dropped as the woman continued to rant at the man. Skye must have taken her down the hall to another room, because the screams, and the swearing, became little more than a faint impression of sound.

Ann leaned back onto the exam table, a little scared by the woman's vehement denial that she was ever going to let the man get her pregnant again. Was the pain that bad?

She reached over to the table where some towels rested, wiped the gel off of her stomach, and rearranged her clothes. A pair of sweat pants and a very large sweatshirt were all she was able to fit into now. Her stomach had become quite large, almost overnight, which was another reason Rager had come.

They were both concerned. Rager's people only stayed pregnant for 6 months and she'd already beaten that timeframe, but maybe her pregnancy wouldn't last as long as an Earthling's would. From what Skye told them, the baby was fine, just big.

"Fuck, I forgot we have medicine for this," Rager said as he came back into the room, his face flushed and clouded with a look of shock. "We have equipment that you'll all need too. I have to make some calls."

Just as quickly as he came into the room he left. All Ann could do was watch and wait for somebody to come back. Skye eventually sent someone back to her room to tell her she could go home. Skye was deep in the middle of a delivery and couldn't leave the woman. Ann understood, so she went out to find Rager.

She finally noticed a heavy weight in her bag, and sure enough, Katy was in there, sleeping in the open largest section of the huge bag's compartments. Ann mainly used it for when she was out gathering supplies, but lately, it was just a convenient bag to keep on her. Especially since Katy had figured out how to pull the zipper down with her teeth.

"You're going to get me in trouble one of these days. Not everybody likes dogs, you know?" Ann stroked the dog's head when she popped it out of the compartment to see why she'd been lifted. The dog licked the tip of her finger, then disappeared back to sleep in the bag. "Lazy little critter."

It was better than the alternative, the hyper puppy that she'd first been given had calmed down and now spent most of her days asleep. Ann was glad she was also a little bit independent, as long as Katy knew where she was, she would run off on her own to walk or play.

"Let's see how long it takes him to notice." Ann stood at the waiting area desk and watched Rager march back and forth. He was talking to some of his people to get some kind of pain medicine and equipment down here from their mother ship.

From the sound of the screams coming from the end of the hall, the pain medicine would be a relief, and the equipment definitely useful. She stood there, patient as always. When he turned to her with a guilty look, she smiled. "It's okay. I know you're helping. Get it sorted, then you can take me home."

He nodded and carried on with the conversations. The woman's screams were stressful and didn't help to ease her mind about what birth would be like. From the sounds of it, it was the most torturous experience a person could have. She'd read a couple of books she'd managed to scavenge early in her pregnancy, and knew what could, would, and might happen. The whole thing didn't seem pleasant, but all the women she knew said that pregnancy and birth were worth the baby you got at the end. She grimaced and turned away from the screams. They would say that though, wouldn't they?

She wasn't sure anything was worth those pitiful wails she heard. Maybe those results weren't typical.

"She won't be screaming like that for much longer. I don't know how it slipped our minds, but we have the means to make this all better. You won't feel any kind of pain like that and we have equipment that makes the process much easier." Rager came up behind her and hugged her close.

She lifted her head, smiled, and kissed his jaw. "That makes it less scary."

"Good." Rager kissed the top of her head and pulled away. "Let's get you home, and away from all that screaming. I've told them to bring some of the pain medicine straight down here to the clinic."

"So, what's it like, this medicine?" She was curious to know. There'd been methods to block pain before the cataclysm, but they came with their own drawbacks.

"It's a cream that's applied to the skin. It blocks the pain signals without causing the euphoria and problems that we had with old medicines. It only blocks the pain, so it won't harm the baby or the mother, and because it's applied to the skin, you don't get some of the problems that might come with injecting at the site of pain."

"That doesn't sound like it would help much, actual-ly," she said as they climbed into the transporter. "Are you sure it actually works? Has it been tried before?"

"Our people use it for a variety of pains. It can't stop the pain, in this case, she's going through some major physical stress, but it will block her from knowing how much pain she's in. That will calm her and make the experience a much better one."

"Will it make her muscles not work?" Ann wasn't exactly sure how to say it. "I mean, will she be able to push the baby out?"

"Of course. It blocks the sensation of pain, not the nerve signals that control the muscles." Rager took the controls and they were soon on their way back to the house.

Ann had planned a couple of stops before they went back to the house, but decided that going home was probably for the best. She was tired, and a little stressed herself, after hearing that poor woman's screams. Rager's news about pain relief was welcomed, but it still didn't calm her mind about what her body would go through during birth.

Women used to die from complications, what if that happened? Would this equipment help with those complications?

"What is this equipment you're having brought down?" She picked at a piece of lint on her sweatshirt, her mind in a whirl.

"It's a robot, basically. A robotic doctor. It can do all kinds of things, scans, monitor, and diagnose problems before they even happen in some cases." He gave her a smile that made her feel better before he turned back to the task at hand. "It's got quite a few different abilities and comes with hands so finely tuned they can pick up a scalpel and do surgery if needed."

"I'm not sure I'm ready for robot surgery," she scoffed and held her hands over her stomach.

"No, it's quite safe, really," he reassured her and reached over to pat her knee. "The same machine has done surgery on many hearts and brains in my world. If it can do that kind of surgery, it can handle anything."

"Wow, yeah, that is pretty good." Brain and heart surgery, she thought, that was impressive. "So, there's not a lot I need to worry about then."

"No, the days when you women have to suffer through birth are over. I'm still not sure why you don't have the same kind of solutions in your world." He sighed with a perplexed look. "Maybe it's because you were so busy making war with each other?"

"From what you've said your people are war-mongers too, Rager!" She protested his dig at her world. "You all even came here as a military force, and still dress as soldiers."

"Ah, but there's a difference. My people are used to defending themselves from constant invasion attempts from outsiders. We also don't make war on each other. We just defend."

"Then you had time to find better solutions to the problems your people face. That still doesn't explain why you came here as a military force." She glared at him, a little angered by the way he always made out that her world was inferior to his.

He might be right, but that didn't mean he had to point it out as often as he did. It had started to annoy her, and she wasn't in the mood for it right now.

He had the good grace to look sheepish at least.

"You're right about that. We wanted to make sure if there were any of you left that you understood we were taking control of the planet," he said without a lot of inflection.

"You invaded us, you mean," she pushed, wanting him to say the words.

"No, not invaded. Well, maybe. We didn't know how many of you there'd be left, and we thought it would likely be void of life. From what we could make of your people, there probably wasn't much chance of survival. But if there were some of you left, we wanted you to know we were in charge."

Rager landed the transporter and the shell opened. She stood up, turned back to look at him, and tilted her head in a way that left little doubt that she was a little bit miffed.

"Well, you made sure of that." She crossed her arms over her chest, or tried to, but ended up with her arms somewhere under her breasts. "I'm going to the bedroom."

"Ann? Why are you angry with me?" He followed behind her, quick to help her down.

"Because you're always putting things down here. Nothing is ever good enough; nothing is up to your level of superiority." She waved her hands over her head, as if to say his level was way over her head. "But, I can tell you this much, Rager. This planet made me, the people made me, and that means that I'm inferior according to what you've said."

"Now that's a jump in logic. How do you get that, Ann? I never said you were inferior." He stared down at her, annoyance in his voice now.

She hadn't wanted to start an argument, but she felt she had to say this, and if he didn't like it, fuck him. She was tired of it.

"No, but everything on this planet is. And by extension, that means I am too, Rager. Don't you get that? Some of your people didn't want you to be mated to me, because I'm inferior to your people. That's what they thought. You only think I'm not because I'm your mate. Otherwise, you'd think me, and soon this baby, aren't equal to you." She turned on the doorstep, her hands cradled around her stomach. "Don't you see? You might not have outright said I'm not equal to you, but you have by the other things you've said."

"Oh." He looked like he wanted to argue with her about what she'd said, but then couldn't think of an argument. "I don't think you're inferior though, Ann."

"Then stop putting everything here down, even if you don't mean to. I know I'm just being emotional because of hormones," she rolled her eyes at herself when tears started to sting to life and swiped the tears away. "But it gets old, you know? And why am I not supposed to think I'm inferior, when all you do is say what I come from and what my world accomplished wasn't good enough? That the people of my world weren't as enlightened as yours, and therefore not as good? I'm a part of that community, you know."

"I do. I'm sorry." He didn't say it petulantly, or with rancor, he just simply apologized. "I should have been more aware of what I was saying. Or not saying, in this case."

"Thank you."

They walked into the house, hand in hand, and Ann wondered, again, if he loved her. She looked up at him, this man that had been a stranger to her when she was mated to him, and felt her heart swell. She hadn't told him how she felt, not in those words. She'd proven her love with her actions, and she just wanted the same in return.

She hadn't realized until that moment just how much it stung when Rager made what he thought were off-hand remarks about her home planet. Yeah, their world had been shit for a lot of people, and it hadn't been a good place for a long time, if it ever really had been, but it wasn't all bad. She'd just wanted him to acknowledge that.

"Want to come upstairs with me?" she asked in a soft voice, a voice that always got his attention.

"Always, Ann."

9

"Jdon't want to see this," Ann whispered to Skye as she walked into the clinic a few weeks later.

Skye came to a sudden halt and looked back at her friend. "What?"

"I'm afraid... you know, the tearing, the screaming, the... mess..." Ann frowned, ashamed to admit any of it, but her fear was stronger than her sense of shame.

"But it's beautiful!" Skye exclaimed; her head tilted now. With her dark skin, the lightness of her eyes was pronounced.

"Beautiful? The books I've read tell me it's a nightmare. And I saw pictures in one book. I thought it was impossible for a baby's head to come out of that area, but I got a full view of what it looks like, and beautiful is the last thing I'd call it."

"I guess it could be frightening, especially if you've never gone through it before." Skye sighed and came up close to Ann to tilt her chin up with one finger. "Look, it's messy, it's sometimes smelly, and sometimes, it's downright frightening, but in the end, there's a baby, and that's why we do this. For that tiny little face and the person that they will grow up to be. The process is hard, it can be really long, and your mom needs you, Ann. That's another part that makes this beautiful. You and your mom will share a bond after this. Come on, she needs you."

"Fine. But if I pass out, none of you better laugh at me."

"We won't, I promise." Skye took her to a room where they scrubbed their hands clean, put on gloves, and then walked towards the birthing room, where Skye had set up the medical robot Rager sent down to them. "I don't know if your mom is early, on time, or overdue, so that robot thing will come in handy. I suspect her babies are breech too, so this could get difficult."

"Okay." Ann took a deep breath, dread a real thing in her mind. Her heart pounded, her head ached, and her mouth was dry. Panic was about to set in, but she took another deep breath and pushed it down.

"Hi, Mom," Ann called out as she walked in to find her mother on the edge of a bed they'd found in a hospital's labor ward. It was designed especially for mothers that were about to give birth, but Skye encouraged all of the pregnant women to do as they pleased while in the throes of labor.

"Hi, baby." Ann's mother, Mary, smiled over at her daughter, and reached out her hand. "Hold my hand. I feel another contraction coming."

"I thought the medicine Rager brought down took the pain away." Ann's eyebrows knitted together as she took her mom's hand. "Why does it hurt?"

"It doesn't, honey, but I can still feel what's happening. It just doesn't hurt, that's all." Mary smiled, a lot more congenial than the woman Ann saw a few weeks ago.

"That's a relief, then," Ann sighed and sat down beside her mother. "Where's Dad?"

"Skye? Have you seen John?" Mary asked and gripped at Ann's hand lightly as her body went tense.

"He's just outside, on the phone. He'll be back in shortly," Skye said and came up to feel Mary's stomach. "Hard one?"

"Yes, and coming closer together too."

"Let's let the robot have a look at you. Can you lie back for me, Mary?" Skye shooed Ann away and Mary lifted her legs onto the bed.

The robot wasn't an android, it was a rather large contraption with four long arms that extended from a large metal box, two of which had delicate mechanisms that acted as fingers, and the other two were empty. They were for exchangeable parts that might be needed throughout whatever procedure the robot's computer deemed necessary. Right now, the two arms took a scanning device out of one of the many compartments contained in the large metal box, and began to scan Mary's abdomen.

"I see the boy is breech, Mary. His little bottom is stuck, his legs over his head. The robot will try to turn him." Skye read from a screen at the top of the box.

The delicate hands of the robotic arms came up to Mary's stomach and gently began to apply pressure in different places. Ann watched, fascinated, as the hands on the robot moved, and then the fingers, to adjust the baby's position with precision. When the baby boy had turned and was facing in the proper direction, the arms pulled back and folded up so that they were out of the way.

Skye laughed as she read out the robot's directions. "Proceed with vaginal birth."

"I'm so glad it gave me permission," Mary laughed with Skye. Ann smiled, still not comfortable being there.

Mary pushed back up to sit on the edge of the bed, but then began to walk around instead.

"Should you be doing that?" Ann was alarmed. What if the baby came out while she was walking around like that? Would she crush its head?

"Yes, Ann. It's alright, darling. I've done this before, remember?" Mary's voice was patient but understanding. "It's scary, I know. I'm a little nervous, even though I've done it before. At least back then I had a lot more knowledge than you do now. Pace with me."

Ann frowned and watched her mother, terrified the baby would just fall out of her mother and smack the ground.

"It's not going to fall out of me, I promise." Mary smirked at her daughter, and Ann sniffed with mock annoyance.

"Fine." Ann put her hands over her own burgeoning stomach and began to pace with her mother.

"I don't know exactly what this robot will do, but I guess I'll have to do most of the work. Back then, we still had a lot of things to worry about, even if our birth went smoothly. Problems could occur after the birth, for baby and mother, but Skye assures me this robot thing is pretty good at what it does."

"It detected a heart rhythm problem with the first lady that gave birth here. It attended to the problem before I even knew there was a problem."

"Really?" Ann remembered Rager said that it could, but she hadn't quite believed him.

"Yes. And it caught a hemorrhage I didn't know about in another case." Skye looked completely confident.

"Good." Ann walked with her mother, and the hours began to pass.

They would walk for a bit, her mom would lie down for a while, Ann played a few dozen games of checkers with her father, until finally Skye said her mother had to decide how she was going to give birth.

"I want to sit up. They had me flat on my back last time, and I hated it." Mary's hair was wet, despite the lack of pain, and her face flushed. "I'd like gravity to help me out a little this time."

"Okay. Let me just settle in." The lower parts of the bed opened and Skye settled down between her mother's legs. Mary's feet were pressed into straps against a panel on the bottom and Skye took a look at what was happening.

"Yep, I can see his little head." She began to give Mary instructions while Ann stood to her mother's right. Her dad was on the left, and they both held Mary's hands as she strained to give birth to the baby. "Rest now."

Mary leaned into Ann, and Ann wiped at her mother's face with a wet washcloth. "You're doing great."

"I think I'm too old for this," she sighed, but then sat back up again. "It's coming again."

"Push for me, Mary," Skye said, and they were right back at it.

There was no screaming, gnashing of teeth or swearing, just the sounds of a woman doing her best to push a baby out of her body. Ten minutes later, cries broke through the silence, and Ann looked down to see a squirmy little body covered in white stuff.

"Ann, clean him up over there," Skye said after she tied the cord and cut it. She handed the baby to Ann, and Ann took him, amazed at how quiet he was.

"Weigh him once you've cleaned him off. And there's an instruction sheet too, that will tell you how to test for problems we need to know about right away."

Ann took the little boy to an area on a counter, where there were cloths to wipe him clean with, and a blanket ready to wrap him in. Ann followed the instruction sheet, gave the results to Skye, and asked what else she should do.

"Put a diaper on him and hand him to your Dad. He wants to meet his son." Skye grinned at Ann, and Ann laughed.

No, this hadn't been so bad. Not nearly as bad as she thought it would be. She put a cloth diaper on the baby and handed him over to John, who stared down at the baby with surprise.

"I was almost convinced this wasn't real, you know, Ann? But here he is." He looked down at the baby with a look of love Ann was quite familiar with. It brought tears to her eyes, and she touched the baby's still damp hair.

"Get ready for the next one. I think you're about to have your hands full."

The little girl came surprisingly quickly, and Ann took her as the robot stepped in for Skye and did another checkup on Mary. "Everything looks good, Mary. You didn't tear, there are no heart problems, and no internal bleeding."

There was a moment of confusion for Ann when the placentas were moved away and covered, but she didn't ask. She didn't want to know about all of that, she just wanted to clean her new little sister off and hold her. She did the same procedure as she'd done with the baby boy and then handed the girl to Mary.

"Here's your new baby girl, Momma," Ann whispered as she handed the girl over. She was bigger than the baby boy, but she was quiet too. She looked around, her hand in her mouth, and then caught sight of Ann. That made the baby girl smile.

"May I still call her Sarah, Ann?" Mary asked, and Ann looked confused.

"What?"

"We talked about their names. Remember?"

"Yes, you can name her Sarah." Ann smiled, glad her mother had decided to stick with that one for the girl. "Are you still naming him Amos?"

"I am. I don't care if you don't like it," Mary said imperiously, but grinned. "I like it and so does your dad."

"Then it's a good name. Sarah Ann and Amos. My brother and sister." Ann grinned, tired, but happy.

Her parents became lost in their new babies and Skye was busy making notes, signing forms, and checking Mary periodically.

"Why don't you head home now, Ann? It's been a long day, and you need to have your dinner. And some rest." Skye gave Ann a look that said the suggestion was an order.

"Fine! Are you sure I'm done here?"

"Yes, I have a helper coming in to stay with us through the night, and your dad is here too. We'll be fine. Take care of yourself. You'll be in that bed in another month or so." Skye pointed out.

"Alright. But if you need me, just call me." Ann picked up her things and prepared to go. She thought, and then turned back. "It's still scary as hell, but you're right, I'm not as worried now. Thanks."

Ann had spent the last couple of days in turmoil. She'd been terrified of what was about to happen to her, to her mother too, and she'd wondered if she kept her legs closed if the baby inside of her would refuse to come out.

She still didn't know what gender the baby was. After that last scan Skye did was interrupted, she and Rager decided to wait to find out. She was glad she had now. She knew that no matter what, she would love her baby. She loved her brother and sister already and they were only her siblings. Her heart had swelled enormously when she'd held each baby, cleaned them, and then checked them over. She had a feeling that would double when it was her own baby.

She went upstairs when she found Rager wasn't home and sprawled out on the bed after a shower. She couldn't get the image of her mom's smile out of her mind and wondered if that's how she'd smile once her baby arrived. Watching a birth actually happen had terrified her at first, but now she knew that she'd focused on the wrong things. The end result was worth all the parts that came before.

She fell asleep and dreamed about making more babies in the future. Dreams that were hot, vivid, and full of the only man she wanted. Rager.

He was always on her mind, even when she had other thoughts to think. He'd introduced her to the world of adult pleasures, and pregnancy hadn't slowed them down. In her dream, Rager guided her, brought her to those same earth-shattering heights he always did, with a smirk that made it all the more intense.

"Wake up, Ann. You've driven me mad for the last 45 minutes." She heard his voice behind her and turned her head.

"How did you get there?" She blinked, swiped at her eyes, and then turned to him. "Oh, I'm awake?"

"Yes, you are, my dear," he whispered against her neck, his hot breath a gentle touch that stirred her already inflamed passions to full life. "I was in a meeting when you started dreaming. I kept getting images of your dreams, and I had to cut it short finally. I wasn't slow about getting here either."

His left hand went to her hip and slid down to grasp at her bottom. He kneaded the muscles there and bit at her neck gently. Ann groaned in response and, her head fell back to invite him in for more.

"You know I want to be gentle with you, Ann, but when you invite me, so very prettily, to bite your neck, gentle is the last thing I want to be."

"Then don't be, Rager. I won't break."

"You might not, but your water might." He nuzzled at her favorite spot while his free hand slid around her hip, to the aching spot between her thighs. "I can't do what I want to with you. Not yet."

"As long as you get me off, I don't care how you do it," she responded, her focus on his fingers now, as they delved beneath the blanket to find her completely naked. His fingers stroked her slick flesh until she sighed in delight.

With an eager move, his head pushed the blanket away from her full breasts to swipe at a tight nipple.

Ann couldn't stop the shiver that raced down her spine as his lips closed over the bud, or the way her fingers dug into his hair to hold him still. Electricity raced up and down in the wake of the shiver, pure pleasure that jolted through her as his lips tugged at her nipple and his fingers stroked at her clit.

His tongue flicked at the nipple, teased her into a delighted purr. When she stretched to push the nipple deeper, he bit down, gently, but enough that she felt it. Her body pulsed somewhere deep inside, and she felt a light sheen of sweat break out on her skin.

He would make her feel good, he would take her worries away, he would make her forget the world, as long as she allowed him to do as he wished. As long as she took the things he offered.

He moved, his tongue a stiff, wet finger that slid into her cleavage and then over, to the other nipple. With a moan of his own, he wetly took the other nipple into his mouth and used it to make her moan for him, all over again. She reached down, frantic to touch him, frantic to know he wanted her, and pushed her hand into his pants. She found him, thick and hard, ready for her. Ann opened her eyes and found the orange glow ablaze in the darkness that surrounded them.

Her heart was a dull thud in her ears as she thought the words she couldn't say.

I love you.

10

His little earthling was on fire tonight. She was always a distraction, a thing he needed, even when he was at work, neck deep in responsibilities. Images of her filled the silences that came at meetings, memories of her taste, of how she moved, took over his mind as men with boring voices presented statistics to him and his teams. When his mind flooded with the taste of her sweet pussy in the middle of a meeting on housing practices, he'd left and come straight home.

He'd been hard from the moment he got in his transporter. Now he was more than hard, he was an aching length of stone that needed the silky depths of his mate's tempting body. He growled as he inhaled her scent, a scent that only she gave off. A scent that could drive him wild if he didn't control himself.

He loved the seductive little sounds she made as her excitement grew, and they were only fuel to the fire that she started in him simply by existing. She was his woman and he was her man, that was that all that mattered for now. He was restless, though, ready for action, but he knew he had to be gentle.

Even before her pregnancy, Ann was more delicate than the women of his world. He had to be careful not to bruise her as his passion consumed him, to not hurt her. Sometimes, she pushed him, drove him over the edge of what he could control, and made him a little rougher than he would normally be. She wanted it now, she wanted to walk that edge between pleasure and pain, but she was close to her time, and he didn't want to leave her sore. Satisfied, but sore. So, he'd wreck her in other ways.

Her hips started to rotate beneath the mound that was her belly, a dance that matched the rhythm of his hand. He let go of her nipple with a rough pop that made her bite her lip. He knew because he moved up to look into her eyes.

They were two soft eyes that stared at him with need, a need that she would only ever show to him. There wasn't a person on this planet that could make her look like that and his dick throbbed in response. His woman.

"You smell so damn good," he said to her and buried

his nose in her hair. He gathered up more of her scent and groaned as his body reacted with more want. More need. Because she made him need her, even when he didn't want to.

"If you could handle me taking my fingers out of you right now, I'd let my tongue do all the work. But I think you'd bite my nose off, so I'll just kiss you instead." His lips moved onto hers swiftly, before she could respond, and swallowed the moan that escaped her open mouth.

Her skin was hot against his, slightly damp, but it only heightened his awareness of her. Even big with his child, she wanted him, and that was something he never wanted to miss.

His brain exploded when her soft lips pressed into his, when her tongue met his immediately to dance in a slow, sensual dance that only made his dick harder. He was certain his dick would be permanently injured if he waited much longer, but he had to get her off first, he had to make sure she got hers before he could even think about letting go.

He slanted himself over her, to press her chest down into the bed as he kissed her deeper, harder, until he thought he'd suck her very soul from her body, the kiss was so deep.

He'd waited too long, ignored those dreams of hers for too long, but he'd have to pay the price. His mate needed him to be gentle, to take his time, and that's what he'd do. Her hand left the front of his pants, to cup his face, and he realized he'd completely blanked on her hand being down there. It had been too much and if he'd allowed himself to feel it, he'd have lost all control.

He wanted that hand back around him, her grip tight as she squeezed him over and over again. She hadn't moved her hand at all, she'd only squeezed, and he missed that now.

Rager felt a tremble go through Ann, felt her hands grip at the back of his head as she writhed beneath him, eager for the rest of his attentions. He groaned a sound of pure torture, but he had to wait.

"Move to the edge of the bed," he said quickly when he broke the kiss, and moved to stand at the side of the bed. He quickly threw his clothes off and guided her around until her feet were on the floor, but her arms were folded on the bed, her head rested on top.

He dropped down behind her, to taste her, to drive himself a little further into hell, but also into heaven. She tasted so good, like nectar he'd been dying to taste. But he had, and now that he had her taste on his tongue, he wanted more.

His hands supported her, held her when her knees went weak from his attentions. But his tongue didn't relent. He stroked her fast, hard, with a will that drove her straight into the heaven she'd craved. She was beautiful, her back arched her head up as she pushed herself up from the bed as the spasms took her.

His nostrils flared with utter delight as her scent grew stronger, more tasty, the longer she came. Her hand came out, reached for him, as her cries began to subside, and her hips stopped moving. She was more than ready to take him now.

He moved, stood up and positioned himself at her entrance. He slid his right palm down her back, and then slid it back up to open her. The point he wanted was there, between the pretty pink petals that hid the entrance to her heaven. The heaven he wanted so much he thought he'd go mad with it.

He put the head of his dick there, just enough to feel what awaited the rest of it. Slick, hot, grasping flesh that would swallow him whole. All he had to do was… push.

Rager groaned, low and long, as he slid himself into her, pushed past the tightness that only eased after he'd fucked into her a few times, and let her have him, all of him.

He stopped when every inch of him sank into her, he contemplated the sensation of being plugged into such a live wire, a dangerous thing that could ruin him if he let it. He'd spend his days inside her if he hadn't taken on so many responsibilities, but he had so he'd enjoy this moment while he could.

She twisted her hips before he'd fully taken his

moment's pleasure yet it didn't matter because his dick throbbed on a wave of pleasure that shook him to his core. He drove her forward with one quick thrust, an order to keep still. An order she ignored.

His will snapped and he finally gave her what she wanted, wild, frantic thrusts that surged deep into her walls, so deep he thought he might not find his way back. He wanted to watch her face, but this was the best way to fuck her now that she was so pregnant. The most comfortable way for her. He lost himself in the feel of her, in the way she wrapped herself around him with her scent, with her sounds, until he felt her explode around him.

As her walls gripped at him, and she screamed his name, he let himself go fully, totally, inside of her. He nearly choked on how good it felt as his toes curled into the floor. His pace became erratic as he slammed into her sweet pussy, over and over, until he was totally spent.

"Fuck." He heard her whisper as she climbed back onto the bed and collapsed on her side. He climbed up beside her and stretched out on his back.

He was going to die because he couldn't breathe, but he didn't care. It had all felt so good, still felt so good, and he floated somewhere, some cloud of euphoria that only she had ever given him.

She reached out in the darkness, found his hand, and he thought the word love.

But love was a human thing, an emotion that they couldn't define but still insisted they felt. They had affection in his world, need, desire of course, but never love. Lately, however, he'd begun to wonder. Had his people cut themselves off from something that the humans found so worthy of the highest of honors.

Earthlings had died for love, had died without love, went to war over love if their ancient tales were correct. Were the things he felt for Ann, the way he felt about Ann considered love? He didn't know. He'd never been in love before, had never felt it, so he wasn't sure what it was.

Was it a need for the other person? A desire to always be near them? To know their thoughts, their desires? If that was love, then he loved her, he supposed. But he had a feeling it was more, it was that warm feeling in his chest when he thought about her, not just the warm feeling he felt when she thought about him. It was the way she took his breath away and made him laugh at the strangest of times. So many things made him think that maybe he did, in fact, love his mate.

But they were earthly notions and not something he'd ever admit out loud. He was the overlord, the master here, and could not be seen as weak. His soldiers would think that he was if they knew, so he'd keep this nonsense to himself.

"I'm going to shower, and then I'll be back, Ann." She only responded with a wave of her hand, and he knew she would likely be asleep again before he returned.

He took a long shower, and when he made it back to bed, his body was relaxed and ready to sleep. He slid in behind her and curled around her body. His hand slid down to her belly, to cup it while she slept.

He still hadn't quite come to terms with the fact that this was his child. He always thought of it as her baby, not his. He'd started to go to her appointments with Skye because she'd asked him to. It had made her child real to him, but it still hadn't crystallized that this was his baby too.

Logic told him it was, that he was about to be a father, but he didn't want to be. Not yet. He wanted another 20 years, maybe 30, with her before they thought about a baby. But humans aged faster than them, and even with the advances in technology that his people had, that technology would not slow down the human aging process enough to give her that much time. Besides, humans didn't have as many eggs to fertilize as women of his race did.

She would run out of opportunities for having babies long before then, even if their technology allowed her to age slower. A flutter of movement beneath his hand, and then a jolt, made him realize the baby had not only just moved against his hand, but had kicked him.

"You little monkey!" he whispered in the darkness but smiled with sudden pride. The baby had kicked him. Her baby. His baby.

He was rocked to his core with sudden awareness. His baby. That was also his child in there. A child he would have to be a father to. That he wanted to be a father to.

She had done this for him as well, he thought as he moved his head to kiss the back of her head. She had done so much for him, without even realizing it. She'd shown him that life didn't have to be his way or no way at all. She'd stood up for herself and her people, on more than one occasion, and had shown him that not all of the humans of this planet were assholes that wanted to destroy the world so they could have everything they wanted.

Katy barked at him, from somewhere on the floor, and he rolled over to pick her up. Lately, she'd wanted to sleep outside, but sometimes she still wanted up on the tall bed to sleep curled up in Ann's neck.

"You're a little monkey too, Katy," he whispered as he put her down in front of Ann. She just swished her tail at him and put her jaw on Ann's neck. She stared at him as if she didn't trust him, even though she knew him.

Then she closed her eyes and licked her lips until she

fell asleep. Even the dog knew Ann and their baby were safe with him. Because, even though Katy might only be a dog, she could sense love and knew when it was around. And, like it or not, Rager was madly in love with that woman. He just couldn't tell her that.

"Will you be alright while I'm gone?" he asked her as he dressed that morning. It was getting closer to her time, and he was worried about her. She rolled over in the bed, her stomach far more pronounced than it had been. She was slower these days, far more tired than she normally was, and it showed in the circles under her eyes.

"I don't think I'll be moving far from the bed today. I feel like my hips are coming out of their sockets," she replied, miserable with the weight on her now.

"My poor darling, it'll be over soon enough, and then we'll have our baby and you'll have your body back." He leaned over to kiss her, took one last look at her face, and left her.

He had a busy day ahead and he was on the way to the first item on the list. There was a new group of humans in one of the holding facilities that had been set up around the sector. There were eight of them at strategic points along a wall, spread around to catch all newcomers before they'd even made it into the sector. Rager had ordered the facilities to be put up after Ann was kidnapped.

He wanted to know if Rex made his way back here, and he'd had time to make it now, if he'd remained on foot. Rager knew that there were no vehicles that could run, except their transporters, so the man would have had to have walked to make it back to their sector. Rager would make sure the man didn't make it into the sector.

Normally he wouldn't go out to the facility to inspect the new arrivals, but these were reported to have come across the rift and down from the north. They could have picked up a straggler like Rex along the way.

Rager had never been emotionally tied to anyone, not even his parents or siblings. That's why it hadn't been hard for him to leave his home planet. He'd been raised with the knowledge that one day he would leave them all behind, and they'd distanced themselves from him. He'd never really known affection or love, not until Ann came to him.

He'd known the touch of a lover, what it felt like to fuck, but he'd never known... love. He still didn't want to admit it to himself, but what he felt for Ann was unlike anything he'd ever known. He loved to see her tired eyes in the morning, how they lit up despite her current exhaustion. He loved the feel of her against him, and his fondest moments were when she fell asleep in his arms, so trustful and carefree.

It wasn't just sex for him. He liked the way she made him think beyond the norm for his people, and to the things her own people needed or believed. He loved the way she made him laugh, too. She kept him company and filled the hours that he knew would have otherwise been filled with boredom.

He needed that, he needed her, and he wasn't about to let some upstart werewolf ruin his life. He made it to the facility in a deserted part of the sector. The place was bare of trees, and the grass was kept cut low. A tall, unscalable fence ran the perimeter, and the facility, made of bricks, stood in the middle. Two storeys high, the facility was a cage at the back of the bottom floor, and the top was a maximum-security lockup with offices.

Rager walked into the reception area and looked around. Security guards stood at the outside of the door and inside, with one stationed at each door. Security was tight and the number of people might have seemed like overkill, but Rex and his revolutionaries had surprised them once already. It wouldn't happen again if he could help it.

"Overlord! I'm glad you're here." A small man with round glasses, a nose too small to hold them up, dressed in a pair of beige slacks and a white, button-up sweater, came toward him. Everyone knew who he was, and nobody questioned him or asked for identification. It simply wasn't necessary.

"Where are they?" The man's name didn't matter. He simply wanted to see if Rex was part of the group, and then get on with the rest of his day. "Have them all lined up for inspection."

"Overlord, we've checked the group for revolutionaries. This trip wasn't necessary..." the man's reassurances trailed off as Rager's eyes blazed in his direction.

Rager had learned to put up with a certain amount of familiarity from the earthlings, he'd even become accustomed to the way some of them thought they knew better than he did or his people, but sometimes, every now and then, he had to remind them of who was in charge. This man only required a look before he bowed his head and made for the locked gate five feet from the door behind the reception desk.

They walked through the gate, and Rager could hear the soft thud of their shoes as they made their way down a hallway made of bare concrete. There were no windows, and the only light came from a single light-bulb stuck into the wall in an awkward place. Likely to keep it from becoming a weapon, he decided as they came up to another gate.

This one required two keys and the man took his time about finding the right ones to insert. Rager was about to kick the man away and do it himself when the gate finally opened. Rager glared down at the much smaller man but didn't say anything.

They finally made it to a partition where two to three dozen people were being kept. They were all stood against the wall, their faces uncovered and held up for inspection. Rager walked up to the gate of the fence and looked in.

"You will be released and housed within a few hours. Once you're cleared, you are expected to obey the rules here. Those rules are in place for your own protection and for the benefit of all. Follow them and we'll all get along just fine." Rager saw women, men, and children stood there, all of them afraid of the alien in front of them.

One man swallowed audibly and Rager looked him over. He looked vaguely familiar but couldn't pick out what it was. He didn't look a thing like Rex, so he dismissed the man from his mind and carried on his inspection. They all looked dirty, hungry, and desperate. They'd left their homes when the news reached them that life on the other side of the rift was much better.

They'd come in the hope of a better future, and he hoped he could give them that.

As long as they stayed out of trouble, they could have the life they dreamed of. If they worked for it, too. Only the disabled were exempt from work in this new world, though that wasn't a law. You didn't have to work, but if you wanted to eat, you would work. There weren't many elderly, but they were exempt as well from the law. A couple of them worked anyway, because it made them feel useful to help rebuild the world. The law, therefore, wasn't based on cruelty, it was just a matter of necessity.

"We have implemented a new law, that isn't in any of the paperwork you'll be given as you leave today. If you leave the sector for a long length of time, you will not be allowed back in. You will be given a tracker, all of you, and we will know how long you leave for. If you accept these terms, you may stay." He didn't see anyone that might be Rex in this lot of newcomers, and he was ready to leave now.

He turned to the small man that ran this facility and pinned him to the floor with his glare.

"Overlord?" the man whispered, fear evident in the way his voice squeaked.

"They will all have trackers, am I clear?" His nostrils flared and his eyes drilled into the man.

"Yes, yes, Overlord. Whatever you say."

"If they refuse the trackers or to answer your questions, they will be put out. Is that clear?"

"Of course, Overlord." The man nodded, his receding hairline a jagged line across the top of his head.

"Good. Have a nice day." Rager nodded his head of black hair and walked away from the man. He closed the gates as he walked out of the facility and back to his transporter. He didn't speak to anyone else, he just headed back to his transporter and climbed in.

He knew, he knew it deep down, that he hadn't seen the last of Rex. And he kind of hoped he was right. He wanted a chance to wipe the floor with that smirky little bastard. He'd terrified Ann, caused an uprising that resulted in a lot of damage to the sector and bred discontent. A chance to pay the fucker back would be great.

Rager put on some music on the mp3 player he'd had repaired for himself, and set a course to take him back to the city hall building used as the main headquarters away from the mothership. It was full of songs from many decades, a compilation Ann had put together for him when she'd scavenged a computer and found it would still come on. It must have been some kind of music buff because there was music on the hard drive that spanned the history of recorded music. It had been a good find, and the fact that she'd taken the time to put a list together for him was… thoughtful.

A smile tugged at his full lips and he put on a pair of sunglasses as he headed into the sun. It wasn't bad being the man a woman loved, the man that Ann loved.

He'd let her down once, he'd allowed a man lower than a bug to enter his home and take his mate. Surprise or not, the attack shouldn't have gotten as far as it did. He'd spent every day since trying to make up for it in some way.

He'd even become used to the idea of being a father. He'd watched Ann's parents as they cooed over their twin children and saw that fatherhood had its rewards. His own father had been absent from his life for many years. He'd send communications, or someone to relay his messages to Rager, and never showed up for the many accomplishments Rager had managed over the years.

He'd started to watch the families around him, saw how the Earth parents put their children's needs first, and wondered if his people had got that wrong. Or perhaps it was a particularity of the earthlings, perhaps their children needed more nurturing than his own people did.

He would do this with his child. The more he felt the baby move within his mate, the more the warmth in his chest grew. He felt something too, pride maybe. He had created life, he and his mate, and they had beaten nature. It would be their job to ensure that that child survived its childhood and became an adult worthy to take its place in this new world. Male or female, the child would be his child. Leadership would likely be a role that that child would take on.

To do that, he had to make sure his new family was safe from all elements. That included Rex and his band of morons. Rager decided to have a new database implemented. All newcomers were already put into a database on the mothership, but he'd have a new one put in place down here. Then there would be two, just in case one was altered in some way.

He had a feeling, a feeling that wouldn't leave him alone. This nonsense wasn't over, and until it was, he would not feel at ease. He'd have the newcomers tracked in that database too. Their movements would be analyzed, and he'd have a new team put together to watch for trouble amongst them all. A new task force. That should do the trick.

It meant more work for him, more meetings, more approvals, but it had to be done. If he wanted to keep his family safe, then he had to make sacrifices of his own. With a determined step that made his bootsteps ring on the tile floor of the City Hall, Rager went to the office he maintained on the ground.

"Good afternoon, John," he said to Ann's father as he walked into the antechamber to his office. "What can I do for you?"

"Mary wanted me to bring this to you. She thought Ann might still be asleep. Poor babe is having a rough time." John followed Rager from the antechamber and into his office. He carried a bag.

"What is it?" Rager asked and sat down behind his desk. He took the bag and opened it up.

"It's some of the clothes Ann made for the babies. They've outgrown them in the last couple of weeks. You might need them for your baby, so Mary wanted me to bring them for you."

"Oh. Thanks." Rager stared down into the bag of tiny clothes. Small little pants, all of soft, cotton materials, shirts, caps, socks, and nightclothes. Rager gulped as he looked at the tiny outfits.

Ann had an entire wardrobe full of them at their house, but he didn't go into the baby's room. It was her domain.

He pulled out a tiny shirt and looked at it. His hand was bigger than the entire shirt. His child would fit into this? It seemed impossible that something so small could possibly be his responsibility. A new worry nagged at him.

Would he break his child with his giant hands? Would he be too rough and not know it?

"It's alright, son," John said softly.

Ann's father was the only person that had ever called Rager that, and he rather liked it. It was only used in private and only sparingly. In times like now, when Rager looked so overwhelmingly unsure. Rager looked at him, a plea in his eyes.

"You sure about that? I could crush the poor child and not even mean to. Look at this." He held his hand out, the shirt against his fingers. It barely touched his palm.

"Instinct will kick in, son. I know women like to talk about a mother's intuition, but I can tell you, fathers have one too. We learn quickly how to control our hands, how to be gentle but firm as we hold our babies. It's scary, I know, but you'll be fine."

"I hope so." Rager looked doubtfully down at the small shirt and sat down in his chair. "Ann will strangle me if I kill our child by accident."

"You won't." He paused and then offered some advice. "Find yourself an orange, carry it around in your hand. Get used to that. By the time the orange is a baby's head, you'll be used to it. Or maybe a tennis ball, if you can find them."

"Thanks, John." Rager nodded his head and began to breathe easier. Maybe this wouldn't be too hard, with his father-in-law's help. He might even be something like prepared by the time the baby came. He doubted it, but there was always hope, right?

$\mathcal{A}$nn put the baby down in a makeshift bassinette and turned to her mother. She wore a smile that lit up her face with pure joy.

"She's just so precious, Mom."

"I know, I can't believe it." Her mother walked over to the bassinette and stroked the baby's hair with her own joyous smile. "I thought you would be our only child, and now, here we are, with two more. It's so different."

"I imagine so, it's been over 20 years and the world came to an end." Ann sighed, her hands on her distended stomach. "And there are two of them."

"Yes, it's easier now, actually. When you were born, I had everybody telling me what to do, what was best for baby, baby this, baby that. I don't think you know, but I had post-partum depression after I had you." Mary sat down beside Ann on the couch in the living room and gave Ann a look of regret. "I tried so hard not to be depressed, but in the end, I had to get help."

"I didn't know. You never seemed depressed to me." Ann turned awkwardly and faced her mother. She'd come over to her mother's house so she wouldn't have to get the babies out, but now wondered how she'd ever get back home.

"I wasn't by the time you were old enough to realize what was going on around you. When I had you, I had women all over the place telling me what to do, how to do it, when to do it. It got to the point that I didn't feel like you were even mine. I'd had you, but somehow it was almost as if I'd rented you and they expected me to give back this perfectly raised adult who'd had everything handed to her. Even men did it, and fuck, by the time you were a month old, I just couldn't take it anymore." Her words came out in a rush and as she spoke her face creased with an ever-growing look of guilt.

"What did you do?" Ann asked and leaned in toward her mother. From the way her mom wouldn't meet her eyes, she knew something had happened, something had forced her to get help.

"I ran away," Mary whispered, her eyes closed, and her mouth turned down in sorrow. "I left you with your father one night, said I was going to get diapers, and I ran away."

"Mom, that must have been really bad then." Ann knew her mother as a loving woman that would never leave her daughter in distress.

"I was gone for a week. Your dad learned a lot that week, mainly about why I'd run away. You had colic from the day you were born, and you cried. Oh, how you cried." Mary shuddered, and Ann knew her mother was reliving those squalls and screams of a baby in pain. "I gave you the medicine the doctors suggested and tried to limit the food I ate, but nothing helped it."

"Dad figured out how to make it better." Ann remembered something, a snippet of information about how he used to rub her stomach every time she ate until she'd go to sleep.

"He did, and he saved us both. I came home, reluctantly, but not reluctant because of you, honey." She rushed to assure her daughter. "I was certain I was about to fail all those women that knew better than me. That I would fail you and you'd hate me. I had no confidence at all. So, I cut all discussion about how to best raise you out of my life, read a few books, and listened to what you had to tell me. Even when most of it was simple observation at the start." Mary smiled at last, her eyes a little shiny.

"I think you did great, Mom, and I'd have never

guessed you thought you'd fail. You are my best friend, really." She hugged her Mom, then told her she had to get home. "Skye's on her way to the house and I really should meet her there."

"It's alright, honey. You get home and rest." Mary stood up to help Ann off the couch, and then hugged her close. "It was never that I didn't want you, Ann. I just didn't know how to cope. So, I learned how."

"Well, I'll follow your lead then, shall I?" Ann said and kissed her Mom's cheek. "You're the best mom in the world, don't you doubt it."

"I won't, see you later, honey." Mary waved her eldest daughter off and sat down with the babies.

By the time Ann made it back home, Skye had arrived and was waiting in her living room. Ann went straight to the couch and slumped down. The winter had settled in, it was rainy outside, and the sky was dark already. There was a roaring fire in the fireplace, and Ann reached her feet out towards it.

"I'm not liking this one bit." Her hand was on her stomach to cradle the spot where the baby kicked. "It's determined I won't have any vital organs left by the time it's born."

"You will, they'll just be… bruised." Skye dropped down to rub her friend's swollen feet and asked how Ann was.

"Just tired, awkward, huge!" Ann let her head fall

back on the deep couch and stared at the black leather it was upholstered in. "I want a new couch. I hate this one."

"Why?" Skye asked, her knuckles deep in between the bones of Ann's feet. "They're so sexy."

"That's why. They won't be once a baby is here." Ann responded and moaned at the odd sensation of pain found but then kneaded into quietness. "That's awesome, Skye."

"I know. I've been giving foot rubs since I was a kid. My mom made me do it."

"You're a saint for touching my stinky old feet. They've been in boots all day."

"They don't stink. You do need some lotion on these heels though, girl."

"Thanks, I'll get right on that." Ann scoffed and moved around until she didn't feel like she'd slide off the couch.

"I've heard a few things this week," Skye said as she sat back down on the couch.

"Like what?" Ann looked over at Skye and saw her friend's face was the normal, lovely face she knew so well now. Hers was puffy and she felt that she barely looked like herself anymore.

"The newcomers are all humans, but they've been given houses closer into the town, not close to the beach like we've been given." She paused, picked up Ann's other foot, and started to knead. "They've all been warned against it, but they're talking about an uprising."

"Not again!" Ann exclaimed, her hands over her face. "Why can't they just go further down the coastline if they want beachfront property so bad?"

"Stupidity, my friend. They've also decided they want their own wolf-shifter servants." Skye waited and watched Ann's response.

"But Rager's dictated that's over and done with!" Ann slid up, slowly, but still up, to stare at Skye with confusion. "The ones that work here now aren't made to, they have their own homes, and their own lives. They have the same benefits and perks that we do. They don't even have to wear uniforms anymore. They aren't virtual slaves anymore."

"I know. There's even a high society developing among the shifters. Your Mom and Amanda are high on that list." Skye smirked, but it was a happy smirk, not a nasty one.

"So, what's the problem?"

"They want the shifters to be slaves again." Skye paused. This time, Ann knew it was something she wouldn't like. "And people of color to join them."

"No!" Ann gripped Skye's hand. "I won't allow that."

"Thanks kindly, white lady." Skye spoke with a mock-high voice and fluttered her eyelashes. "I know you didn't mean it like that, but yeah, that was wrong."

"I didn't mean because I'm white, Skye!" Ann was hurt and it showed in her face and voice. "I meant because I'm the overlord's wife. Which, ahem, probably isn't any better."

Ann's cheeks turned red and Skye laughed at her discomfort. "Calm down, my fair lady. I know you meant well. But yeah, that shit's scary."

"Well, we won't allow it, will we?" Ann included Skye in that we this time. Skye nodded. "But I will speak to Rager about it. Thanks for letting me know."

"My pleasure. Now, if I'm not mistaken, I've heard the door open, which probably means the Overlord is home. I shall take my leave." Skye gave a courtly bow before she ran back to hug Ann. "I love you, sister."

"I love you, sister." Ann meant it, and knew it shone in her eyes just how much she meant it. She could almost feel the love beaming out of the orbs. "Bye."

"Well, bye to you, my princess," Rager said as he came in and took the place Skye had just left. "That was Skye leaving in a blur, was it?"

"Yes. I guess she was in a hurry to get home." She leaned back against the arm of the couch and looked him over. "How was your day?"

"Cold. Wet. Miserable. Better now that I'm home." His hand rubbed at her legs, bare beneath the long rusty red skirt she wore so she didn't have to try to fit into pants. "How are you?"

"Well, Skye's just told me the new arrivals that came in earlier this week are causing problems."

"Oh?" he asked, but she could see he was more interested in her legs than her words.

"Yes. They want to make the shifters slaves again." His hand slid up her calf, over her knee, and almost distracted her, but she carried on. "And people of color."

"I'll soon sort that out, don't you worry." His hand went higher, skimmed up to her thigh and nudged until she opened for him. "For now, I want to forget today, and find somewhere warm and relaxing to be."

"Well, if that's what you're after." She let her legs fall open and laughed as he bent over to tilt her hips up to his face. His tongue came out to stroke her, and she nearly lost her mind.

She felt fat, clumsy, and unattractive, but Rager came home every night and made it clear she was more beautiful than ever. His tongue danced along her skin now, a tease she knew wouldn't last long. Being pregnant had increased her nerve sensitivity, and it only took him seconds to make the world go dark for her.

She clutched at the couch, but it was too rigid to claw into. She panted his name, then she screamed it as he took her high, just before he took her. It was fast, satisfying, and only a prelude to the things he'd do later. Pregnancy had not only made her more sensitive, it made her more... aroused. And he loved to see how much he could make her scream his name in one night.

When they were finished, she slid off the couch and down to the floor to sit in front of the fire, a blanket over her shoulders.

"I'm worried about these newcomers, Rager," she told him, and he sat up to zip his pants back up, but he didn't replace his lost shirt. He never did feel the cold quite like she did.

"Don't worry, darling, I'll take care of it." His feet stuck out of the bottom of his trousers, strong manly feet but tipped with toes that were almost... pretty. Still masculine but not those ugly peanut-looking things some men had.

"I wish you didn't have to, though. I wish people would give up those old notions." He came to sit beside her, and they both stared into the flames.

"That's our job, Ann. To make them see new ways, to accept new things. We can't just expect people to change an entire lifetime of ideas because of one cataclysm and a mini ice-age."

"Isn't that kind of the point though? Things might not have been so bad for us, if we'd all worked together, been more prepared, learned to listen to what the planet was telling us."

"You're right, yes, but, well, people are strange, no matter what planet they come from. Take the men that wanted me to not mate with you. My men. They knew better, they knew you weren't inferior, but in their heads, you were. Not fit, and not acceptable. They're now on a prison planet for their crimes." His voice was rough, but he held her gently, with care.

"Good. I hate to be that way, but they helped Rex, and that is just wrong to me."

"Exactly. Now, are we going to eat dinner, or are we going to stare at the flames all night?"

"I sent the staff home. We can have what they left for us, or I can bring something in here for us and we can camp?"

It was too cold to sit outside now and eat, the fire made it feel a little more romantic and a little bit like being outside to Ann.

"You stay here, I'll heat dinner up and bring it in here. You don't need to be up again until we go up to bed."

"Thanks, baby," she called out to him as he left her there.

He wasn't anything like she thought he'd be that first day. He was gentle, kind, and he took care of her. Like she was precious to him. Neither had yet to say the 'L' word, but she suspected it was there for them both. Rager was an alien though, and from what she'd observed of them, love and affection weren't high on their list of things to have or show. The fact that he was affectionate, caring, showed far more than she'd seen from most of them. She hoped they all found the kind of happiness she'd found with her mate, though. The world would be a much happier place if it had. Even if Rex was still out there in the world, somewhere.

13

"Who is this guy, again?" Rager asked and Ann rolled her eyes at him. She'd told him a few times already.

"His name is Greg Alleman, he's a country music singer. Kind of blues mixed with country. He's a really good entertainer." Ann gripped her fingers around Rager's hand and leaned into him with a soft laugh. "You'll like him, I promise."

"You just want to meet him." Rager teased her with a playful grin. It was a new thing from him and showed a playful side she hadn't been aware of before.

"Sure, I want to meet a still gorgeous former country music god like this." She waved around her stomach and the rest of herself. "You might love me like this, dear, but I doubt anybody else does."

They laughed together as they walked to the back of

the makeshift stage and went through to his dressing room. Rager knocked and when the man called for them to come in, Ann followed her husband, her hand cupped in his. She was nervous but excited too and it showed in the way she couldn't stop the grin that spread over her face.

"Hi," she said shyly, and walked further into the room, her hand held out. "I'm Ann and this is my mate, Rager."

She didn't need to explain that Rager was the Overlord of the world now, everybody that came into the sector knew it. She stared up at the tall man and noted he still wasn't as tall as Rager.

"Hi there, I'm Greg Alleman, it's nice to meet you both. Won't you have a seat?" He waved at some chairs sat around the small room and they all moved around until they were settled.

"How did you manage to survive?" Ann asked, even though she knew most of the story.

"My crew and I managed to fill up my tour bus with food and supplies, and then we went up to a cave system one of the guys knew about. We holed up in there and scavenged when we could. We found a place in there where it stayed a pretty constant temperature, one we could all live with, and just tried to survive. There was some kind of hot spring that flowed above the rocks and it really helped us to keep warm. Food became a problem, but we had a lot of beans and rice, canned goods, things like that."

"What did you do when you weren't scavenging?" Rager asked, curious as to how they'd spent the many hours of the day.

"We built an entire apartment complex in there, if you can believe it. Then we raided libraries for books, magazines, things like that. Games that we became bored with after a few years. We did a lot of exploring of that cave system too. That kept us occupied most of the time. It was too cold to go outside, and well, we just did whatever we could. I wrote a lot of songs and even a book that I burned. I didn't think it would ever see the light of day, and well, you guys came along and I thought I'd better keep my secrets a little while longer." The country legend, still handsome in his early 40s, tilted back the black cowboy hat he wore, and stuck his feet out in front of him as he leaned back against the ladder back chair he was in.

Greg wore a denim, button-up shirt and a pair of jeans that he must have had for years, they looked so soft and well-worn. He was handsome, she'd give him that, and he could sing a song that could tear her heart apart, but he didn't hold a candle to her mate. She smiled, some of the amazement blunted now. Not because she didn't like him, but because she realized he was just a regular guy with a wonderful talent.

"Why did you come here?" Ann asked the question she always asked newcomers when she met them.

"I heard civilization was coming back. The guys I holed up with, they stayed back in Wyoming, but I thought I'd come out here, see what was happening." He stroked his left hand at his back, and Ann knew it was the tracker that bothered him. It was half an inch long and the size of the tube in a ballpoint pen, but you knew it was there, even if you couldn't feel it, or touch it. "It's been good so far."

"We're glad to have you. And thanks for putting on this little break for us all. Everybody has worked so hard, and the winter has already been long, even if it's only barely started. It will make a lot of people smile. We appreciate that." Rager held his hand out to the man, and they all stood up.

"It's my pleasure, Overlord." Greg looked Rager dead in the eye and gave him a friendly wink. "I like what you're doing here, and I plan to stick around for a while, so if there's anything else I can do just let me know."

"We will. This is enough for right now. I hope it's as fun for you as it will be for us." Rager eyed the man's hat for a moment and then he took Ann's hand.

"It was great to meet you, Greg. Thanks again." Ann waved as they left the room to head out to the front of the stage. There was a cordoned area just for them, and Rager headed for that spot with her in tow.

"He's a nice guy," Rager mused, and then looked at Ann. "Do you think I need a hat like that?"

"A cowboy hat? Whatever for? You don't ride horses." Ann's soft laugh made him smile.

"He doesn't either, but I thought it might help me to blend in." He tried that playful act on her again, and she could have melted into a puddle.

"You're going to kill me with how awesome you are, you know?" She made a face at him and then turned away. "Besides, between your height and your eyes, darling, you will never be able to blend in. Even among your own people."

She meant it offhand, but when she glanced over at him, she knew her words cut him to the bone. He would always be different, and normally that didn't bother him. Lately, however, he'd wanted to find some kind of acceptance from her people as more than just the leader of the known world. She patted at his back and slid her arm around his waist.

"It's not a bad thing, babe. I love looking at you, you know?" It was as close as she could get to 'I love you' without saying it.

"I suppose so." He guided her to a chair that had obviously been brought from someone's home, it was a recliner after all, and settled down. It was patched in places, but she didn't care, she was off her feet and comfortable.

"There's water and snacks in that cooler there." Rager pointed at a blue plastic box with a white lid. "And Jake's bringing us a meal later."

"That's awfully kind of him," Ann said and settled deeper into the recliner by pulling the foot panel up.

The concert started then, with the leader of the village on the stage to welcome them all. It wasn't in Ann's father's sector, and she wasn't sure who this man was.

She brushed down the ankle-length, emerald green, empire-waisted knit material of her dress, readjusted the long, cream-colored wool coat she wore, and wiggled her toes in long, black leather boots with flat soles. It was the prettiest outfit she could come up with for a concert that was staged in the evening. It was probably too cold for the event, but people were already arriving, and like her, they'd brought blankets with them.

Skye showed up, and then Meg, and they took the seats that were placed around for friends and family of the highest-ranking couple in the land. Ann's parents came as did Rex's parents, and they took seats in the small area in front of the stage with the rest. Everybody had brought their own drinks and snacks, and they all shared bites and sips of their drinks.

The people had all started to blend their own fruit juices and drink concoctions. Ann, Mary, and Amanda had been working on wine for a while and Mary had brought two bottles of their first batches. It had taken a lot of reading, practicing, and a lot of patience, but they'd finally managed to get a crystal-clear liquid from a brand of grapes that almost resembled Concord grapes. It was a sweet wine, best for desserts, but they were all proud of what they'd created. Ann had only tasted a spoonful so far, but she liked the taste.

The night wore on, people came and took their seats, and Greg kept everybody entertained with his songs. He'd managed to put a small band together, and they all played well together. Ann remembered most of Greg's songs, and some that he'd borrowed from other performers, and she was able to happily sing along with him.

The night grew colder and she pulled two blankets over her body to stay warm. The songs continued after a short break and Greg sang a song that had the entire crowd singing along with him. Ann smiled and snuggled quietly there, at peace with the world. It was a lovely moment, and one that Rager and his people had given to them, whether it was stated bluntly or not.

If they hadn't come, the number of people that were there now would have dwindled eventually, until there were none left. Ann was well aware of that fact. She knew they could have survived several more years in the bunker, and others might have survived even longer, but without the aliens, the Earth wouldn't have warmed up. Life wouldn't have sprouted back into existence once the ice melted. This wouldn't have happened.

Greg finished the song to a long round of applause and sat back on the stool he perched on as the crowd stood up and began to cheer. "Now, let me tell y'all. I was born into a poor family, I used to sing at county fairs and on local bars until a fella decided to make a star out of me one day. I've sung a lot of songs, but that one is special. With that said, I hope you think this one is too."

He began to strum at his guitar and played a rather complex little introduction that had them all silent as they watched the man play. Rager, right beside Ann, took her hand and held it as the song's introduction ended and Greg began to sing. It was a song about the cataclysm, a ballad really, about all the people lost, but as Greg sang, and the song's pace picked up, he sang about hope, the new possibilities, and it became a ballad about how the people that remained would rise to face the challenges.

It was a breathtaking song, long, but full of hope that ended the night on a positive note. It stirred the audience to their feet for a second time and whistles and cheers rang out around the small former parking lot that was now a meeting place. Ann would have waddled up to her feet to clap along with everyone else if Rager hadn't stopped her with pressure on her hand.

"You need to stay off your feet, Ann. Skye says you're too close to be standing on your feet for too long," Rager reminded her gently.

"I know," she said softly. "I just can't get comfortable, and Greg's song made me forget, for just a little while, how uncomfortable I am."

They made their goodbyes and Rager took them home. "Everybody talked about how nice it was to have live music."

"I heard that a time or two." She nodded as she spoke, and thought about how there'd even been dancing. "Maybe the next time we have a little concert like that we'll be able to dance along with everybody else. I'm too big to dance now, but I would have loved it."

"Next time, Ann. You'll be able to dance the entire night away then. For now, it was nice just to have a moment of fun."

"I didn't think that would ever happen again, you know? At least not for a long time. A concert, by a very famous artist from the past. It was just… heaven, really." She grimaced at her own star-struck sentimentality. "Silly of me, of us all, but it was nice to have a night like that. It almost felt like some kind of normality had returned."

"But hasn't it, Ann? People go off to work, make their

way home, celebrate their days together, deal with bureaucracy, and are building families. There were three new babies this week alone. Life goes on, wasn't that a song from your past?"

"More than one song, I guess, when you think about it." She had to agree. "And I guess it's true. Life goes on. We had a lot of help from your people, but yeah. Life goes on."

"We'll make the best of it then." Rager's pride in his part in the renewal of life on Earth was evident in his voice. They'd managed to melt the ice, encourage plants and animals to come back to life, and even worked to decrease the time it took for plants to bear fruit. Animals were also treated for a while to become adults much faster than they were used to.

Now, there were fields to the south, where it was still warm, and vegetables grew with plentiful joy. Animals could also be seen along the countryside, grazing on the grass as the days grew colder. Cows were there for milk, deer, pigs, and chickens were raised on farms run by the sectors. Everything was proportioned, accounted for, so that the families in each sector had enough food, and a variety of choices in food.

People were still eating some of the canned and dried goods that weren't toxic looking, but for the most part, everything was being renewed. Things from the old world that could be useful were brought back to life, while others were repurposed for other things. People made do, learned new skills, and relearned old ways in order to bring prosperity to the sectors.

Ann's life was far richer than she'd thought it could be when she'd first entered the bunker all those years ago. As Rager drove them home, she felt hope that her child, secure in her belly, would grow up in a world worth living in. If only they could keep it going in the right direction.

14

"I'm sorry, ladies, I'm not able to do much walking around today, or standing," Ann said from her place on the couch. It was another social gathering of the female mates of the sector's leaders. Today wasn't the best day for it, though.

Ann was experiencing some stretching, tearing sensations in her hips and lower back. This created pain that left her wincing, and more than one of the women present looked at her with concern.

"Just the stretching," she assured them all with a grimace of a smile. It was the day after the concert, but 24 hours closer to her due date. Whenever that was. "Meg's going to be presenting us with a, um, presentation on the clinic, ladies. An update, if you will, on how it's progressing."

"Thank you, Ann." Meg stood up, a small woman that hated to be in the spotlight, she went to stand in front of the women by a small chalkboard on a tripod that she'd brought in with her earlier. "If you'll look here..."

The women all turned, and Meg started to write numbers on the board. "We've treated this many people this week. An increase from last week, and a clear sign that more people are coming to trust the care we can give them. We're certainly not up to the standards of specialists or hospitals, but we're gaining knowledge every day and showing progress."

Meg gulped, but she kept talking, despite the way her voice trembled as she looked around. She looked like the last chicken, trapped in a room by a horde of starving dogs.

The women weren't that brutal, Ann thought with a silent laugh. She kept her face straight and gave her attention back to Meg.

"Now, we want to start screening for psychological problems that some of our people might have to deal with. A psychologist came in with the last group of newcomers, and he's offered his services to the sector."

The women tried not to show it, but they were all interested in this. Each of them had their own problems, and most had learned to adapt to their new lives, but it had been a brutal life since the cataclysm. They could probably all take a turn on the doctor's couch.

"That sounds like a very good idea, Meg," Ann volunteered. "I think we should make sure we start this new world on the right foot. There should be no shame in mental or physical ailments that might limit some of our fellow citizens."

Ann was no speechmaker, but she hoped that worked. That should help to eliminate any stigma from the old world. She hoped.

"Now, I'd like to do a little presentation on wellness checks."

Ann's back decided to start a rather vigorous impersonation of a boa constrictor and started to shrink around her spine at that moment. That's what it felt like anyway, she thought as she sucked in a lungful of air.

"Put a pillow behind your back, dear." An older woman with a kindly face handed Ann a pillow. She was on the other end of the couch and had noticed the way Ann flinched. "I had this with both of my girls, awful back pains that everybody just ignored. It's like people forget how miserable you can be when you're this pregnant."

"It's not exactly flowers and hearts, is it, this pregnancy business?" Both Ann and the other women kept their voices down as Meg continued to speak.

"I'm lucky to be past that business, and still married to my husband after 38 years. It's not exactly flowers and hearts, no, but it can bring so much joy when you have the baby with you." She was a kindly looking woman with white hair and soft gray eyes.

Ann smiled and shoved the small throw pillow in her back. It helped a little, enough to make sitting there for another hour bearable. The women eventually all filed out and Meg checked on Ann.

"I saw you struggling. It's a shame we can't give you pain medicine, but we don't really have any. Only that stuff Rager keeps bringing down for us, and I'm not sure how addictive that stuff is."

"But it doesn't get you high," Ann protested, but not with anger. She was just resigned to being in pain at this point.

"I don't mean it like that. I guess I should say how quickly we build up a tolerance to it. We want to make sure it works really well when you go into labor. Or need it for some other type of pain."

"I understand." Ann wanted to whine, but she wasn't a whiner. She just took a deep breath, closed her eyes, and pretended the pain was slowly ebbing away.

"Just keep breathing, my love," Meg said and patted Ann's arm before she left.

Ann pushed herself up awkwardly, but managed to get up. She was going to bed. She might not be a whiner, but this was painful. She asked the woman that kept the house clean, Jean, to bring her a bottle of hot water wrapped in a towel, and made her way up the steps. It took her longer than she thought it would and wondered if it was time to move to a bedroom downstairs.

Katy, asleep in the pocket of her loose hoodie, protested with a whine, but Ann patted at the small dog and carried on her climb. By the time she got to the top, she was ready to collapse on the floor, but she managed to make it to the bedroom. She'd been in so much pain earlier, she'd slipped on black jogging pants and a black hoodie instead of dressing properly.

"That's good enough to call jammies, isn't it, Katy?" Ann asked out loud, but the dog just crawled out of her pocket, pushed her snout into the hair at the nape of Ann's neck against the pillow and collapsed back into sleep.

"You're not even pregnant, what's your problem?" Ann didn't get an answer to that either, and she soon fell asleep.

She woke up later to find the sun had gone down, and Rager wasn't home. He'd sent her a message on her communicator to say he would be very late, and not to wait up. She buzzed down to the kitchen and asked them to bring up dinner, and when they did, she thanked the servants profusely. They'd saved her a walk down that long flight of stairs.

She ate in bed, her music on, which was probably why she didn't hear someone outside. She didn't notice anything at all until a hand slammed against one of the glass panes of the double doors. Ann shrieked, which surprised even her, and scrambled out of the bed.

"Ann!" a strangled voice called.

Ann knew that voice, recognized it immediately, and ran from the bed.

"Skye! What's happened?" She opened the door and got down on the floor to cradle her friend's head in her lap. "Jeffrey? Are you there? Call Meg, quickly. Tell her Skye is hurt and to bring one of the medical kits we put together."

Her communicator had automatically dialed the butler when she said his name with her mouth close to the device. The man, tall, slim, and always officious, assured Ann that he would.

Ann looked over Skye and couldn't make anything out. There was blood all over, so much blood, and every part of her face was swollen, marked with purple and red bruises that look painfully sore. Skye's eyes were almost swollen shut, her lips were busted in several places, and Ann was certain some of her facial bones were broken. Even her nose looked skewed.

"Are you hurt anywhere besides your face?" Ann tried to examine the other woman lower down the body, but was afraid to let her head go. She pulled up the woman's shirt, as far as she could go, and could see what might be stab wounds, with fresh blood oozing from the thin lines.

Ann wanted to turn Skye over, but was afraid that it might cause further injury. "We need a neck brace, something to stabilize your neck, and a backboard. Fuck, where is Meg at?"

Ann had started to read up on emergency medicine when she became bored with reading maternity books. She'd realized, as she read the books, that medicine might be her calling. She wasn't ready to commit to anything yet, not until after she was used to being a mommy, but maybe she'd have a try after the baby was a couple of years old. In the meantime, studying books was free.

"Ann, I've brought you our first aid kit," Jeffrey called with a knock at the door. The normally unflappable man's eyes went wide and he stumbled a little as he saw the state of the now mumbling Skye.

"Ann, you have to…" her words cut off with a strangled sound and she groaned pitifully. Jeffrey knelt down on the floor with the marooned Ann and tried to help by digging through the first aid kit.

Skye had gone quiet, but she suddenly sat up, looked at her friend, and spoke.

"Ann, the revolutionaries are back." Her eyes spun in her head for a moment, and then, she passed out.

"Fuck, that's bad. That's very bad," Ann muttered and held her communicator up to her mouth. "Rager?"

"Ann?" he responded immediately. "What's going on?"

"Skye's been attacked from the looks of it. She says the revolutionaries are back. I don't know how, and she's just passed out, but I'll do my best to find out what's happening."

"Lock the doors, now!" Jeffrey moved when he heard Rager's order, and used his own communicator to spread the order. "Lock it down, Ann."

"We are." Her hands shook almost as much as her voice when she put her arm down. She reached for Skye's neck, felt the pulse, and breathed a sigh of relief. Skye's pulse was steady and strong at least.

Meg soon arrived, escorted in by a soldier that Ann hadn't even known was there, and began to examine Skye. "Is there anyone that can help us move her? We need to get her off the floor."

Ann called for help and two more soldiers appeared. They moved Skye into a smaller bedroom and Meg began to pull off Skye's clothes. "I don't think any bones are broken, she doesn't look too bad. This is a superficial wound from what I can tell."

Meg examined what Ann had thought was a stab

wound. Ann looked closer and could see now that the wound had stopped bleeding and wasn't as deep as it had looked at first. Ann watched as Meg started an IV line, attached a glass bottle of saline water they'd prepared at the clinic, and started to clean Skye's face up.

"We'll need to get her to the clinic when Rager says we can leave, but for now, she's going to have to deal with no scans. This is about all I can do until he lets us go out of the house."

"Did you give her the pain medicine?" Ann asked, worried that her friend would be in pain.

"It's in her IV line now." Meg watched Skye closely as she washed away the blood and dirt, but the other woman didn't respond. "I think there might be some problems internally, but I'm not sure."

"Rager will let us out soon, I hope," Ann assured the medic.

"I hope so."

Skye remained unconscious for another hour before she opened her eyes and coughed. "Where am I?"

"One of my guest rooms, Skye," Ann said and stood up to look down at her friend. "How are you?"

"I'm not in pain, so I guess Meg is here somewhere?" Skye looked around but didn't see anyone, so she looked back at Ann. "I have to tell you something."

"It's okay, don't talk. You said the revolutionaries

were back." Ann hushed her friend until Skye settled her head back onto the pillows.

"Good. I couldn't remember…" her voice trailed off and she was asleep again.

"Did I hear Skye?" She'd been in the bathroom connected to the bedroom and came out quickly.

"Yes, but she's asleep again." Ann sat back down in her chair; her nerves frayed as the minutes passed. They needed to get Skye to the hospital, fast.

"He's only doing what he thinks is right, Ann. Don't be too upset," Meg said as she checked the supplies in the kit she'd brought one more time.

"I know, I'm just frustrated. There's been no sign of any of them. He needs to let us out."

"He will when he's certain it's safe. Not just for you, but for all of us."

"You two are so noisy," Skye coughed out and sat up. "I'm fine, just battered."

"Well, that's an improvement." Ann gaped at her friend. She'd been at death's door a moment ago, and now she was wide awake? What had happened?

"I would say," Meg responded, her face a mask of surprise.

"What's going on?" Skye asked, confused.

"You were passed out, now you're wide awake and sitting up," Ann spluttered, still surprised.

"I think I'm part shifter sometimes, I heal so well,"

Skye informed them and pushed a pillow up behind her back. "I don't know why, but I always have healed well. It's sometimes sudden like that too."

"But you aren't a shifter at all. They checked everybody." Meg was still in stun mode too; Ann could tell by the way she kept staring at Skye.

"We can study it later. Do tests, whatever. Did I tell you what happened at all?" She looked between the two women but neither responded. "About the revolutionaries?"

"Yes. But not what happened to you." Ann dismissed the news as old and pushed on for new information.

"Well, I saw one of them, the old ones from the last uprising, and followed him back to one of the places at the edge of the new sector. The one with the fewest people?" When both women shook their heads, Skye continued. "They've dug a hole under the fence there, and they're letting people in."

"No!" Ann exclaimed, and knew there'd be trouble. Why did people always have to cause trouble? "And they saw you?"

"I fell off a trash can I'd stood on to look into a window. They heard me, came out, and proceeded in a major attempt at stomping my face in." She indicated her face and then continued. "I managed to play dead and they left me in the alley. But not before I saw who the ringleader was of the face-kickers."

Skye paused and Ann felt her stomach go tight.

"Who was it?" But she already knew. Dread filled her and anger quickly followed.

"Rex. Rex was there with a load of brand-new followers. We're in trouble."

15

"The soldiers are in place?" Rager asked the computer onboard the mothership. His ears were perked up, to listen for its reply, even though he knew the sound came from the sides. Everyone responded the same way when they awaited a response from the system, their ears perked upwards.

"They are, Overlord," came the softly spoken reply. Rager knew it wasn't actually spoken, nor was it a real voice, it was a simulation of the computer system, letters and sounds put together to produce responses that could be understood by anyone. "I have located the place where your targets have taken sanctuary, Overlord. Do you want me to destroy it?"

"No, I want to be there. Call me a transporter and prepare the soldiers. We're leaving now."

Rager stomped down the passageway, anger, rage, in

every step he took. He could hear the noise of soldiers getting into transporters as he made it to the large area at the bottom of the ship where the transporters were kept and maintained. Small vehicles left, on the way to the location of the latest troublemakers. Rager got into one, filled with soldiers, and they followed the vehicles that had already left.

When they landed, a good half mile away from the abandoned building where the revolutionaries hid, they formed into ranks. Rager was in the lead, a helmet with a face shield in place. Like the other soldiers, Rager wore the lightweight armor that would protect him from the human's weapons, if they had any, and would prevent their alien technology from doing them harm. The soldiers could be knocked down, but their armor could not be penetrated, nor could the helmets or the face shields.

In the last battle, the aliens had learned to wear the armor that they'd left in the ship. There'd been a lot of doubt that the humans could have found any weapons that could harm them. There'd been an arrogance there that they soon regretted. They'd lost two of their soldiers. This time, that wouldn't happen.

"Let's move in." There were speakers and microphones in the helmet, controlled by buttons on the side. Rager left his mic open so that he could send out orders and started to march towards the small brick building situated in a small section on the outskirts of the city.

The small building stood between two much taller buildings, but all seemed to be around the same age. Rager counted six floors, which meant they'd have to sweep a lot of rooms, but every single room would be inspected before he would declare the building clear.

"Move into the first floor, four of us will clear it. The rest of you head up, four to each floor." Rager told the soldiers, made up of women and men, and walked up to the door. They all knew the procedure by now, but he repeated it anyway, just in case.

It was still dark and there were no lights in the windows, but Rager could see where the door was. He took one deep breath, pictured Ann's face, and then kicked the door in with one swift punch of his leg.

He flicked the flashlight on his weapon to the on position and barked out orders. "Get on the ground, get on the ground now!"

People screamed, scrambled, and moved to obey the orders given. Rager saw men, women, and a few he couldn't identify as he swept the area in front of him with his weapon. People obeyed the orders swiftly, but he spotted a few making their way to the back doors. A couple made it out before he and his soldiers could get to them, and Rager sent the two soldiers behind him after them.

He came back once he was certain the three rooms on the ground floor were clear and headed up. He heard the sound of Earth-made gunfire and quickened his run up the flight of stairs. By the time he got up there, explosions had started to go off outside, and Rager could hear screams of pain. He had one hundred soldiers with him. If one lost their life, these humans would pay.

He quickly spotted the shooter from the second floor and went after him as the man ran from the alien soldiers. The man ran right into him, bounced away, and Rager swiftly kicked the shooter in the knee to drop him to the ground. He couldn't see any more targets so he headed up to the third floor. He wasn't even out of breath when he paused there. His soldiers gave him the thumbs up so kept climbing. He found his soldiers in a back room, waiting on orders. Someone was holed up in a room there.

"Blow it open if you have to. Get them all out," Rager said softly and waited.

The soldiers kicked in the door and when gunfire rang out, used their weapons. When the smoke cleared, there were three dead earthling males on the floor, and the room was quiet. "Good."

He moved up to the fifth floor and was about to go search for his soldiers when an explosion blew the top floor off the building. The entire structure trembled, and the floors started to give way just as debris began to rain down on Rager.

He made it halfway down the steps before a large beam knocked him down and the floor completely gave way. He didn't make a sound as he fell, down and then further down. The impact was dampened by his suit, but he still felt the jolt as his body came to a sudden stop. It knocked the breath out of him, and he sucked in, trying to get air to go into his lungs.

The whole world span around, and then went dark. He came to when someone punched a fist directly over his heart and shocked him back to awareness. "Fuck!"

He gasped in air, sat up, and pushed debris off his legs.

"That was some wave you caught, Overlord." A soldier, a female from the sound of it, said and held out a hand to help him up.

"So, it seems. Status report?"

"All of ours are accounted for sir, but we lost a few of the targets. They're crushed on the first floor, where we'd gathered them to await transport."

"Not a loss, then." It saved him the time of giving them a trial and the resources to punish them.

"No, Overlord. We just have to deal with the ones outside now."

"Good. Has Target One been located?" Rager had given Rex the designation before the mission began.

"No, Overlord, he has not. He's not been spotted among the ones setting off the bombs now either."

"Alright. This is under control; I'll leave you all to it." Rager could see the battle was all but won, the last hold-outs would be dealt with. He needed to go home, protect his mate.

That was when he heard new explosions, from the area where they'd left the transporters. He ran to the area and fell to the ground as someone knocked him down. He grunted as he hit the ground and rolled over. A man, a very tall man but still an earthling, stood over him with a piece of timber in his hands, one of the timbers from the building if Rager wasn't mistaken.

He didn't think about it too long, he just brought his weapon up, fired, and turned to push himself off the ground. He'd taken two steps when the ground before him vaporized and a wave of energy knocked him right back down.

"Bastards," he muttered, but picked himself up. His helmet was scratched, but he could still see through the dark pane.

More of his soldiers flooded by him and the group of four that had some kind of grenade launcher were taken out. He made his way to his transporter and quickly pulled it into the sky. He could see below that the group now dead on the ground and the group that was still fighting near the building was finished. He couldn't see any more activity and headed in the direction of home.

His gut told him that's where he needed to be. It had been a long fight, but most of the battle was done. His soldiers would deal with that. He had to make good on a promise he'd made to Ann. He pushed the transporter as fast as it would go and called ahead to the soldier at the front door.

"I'll be there in two minutes, what's the status there?"

"All clear, Overlord. No sign of anyone or anything around the house."

"Good. Kill whatever comes near it. There are still targets on the loose." Rager could see the lights on the front of the house and breathed a sigh of relief as the lights became brighter. Everything was fine.

His mate was slow and cumbersome these days, and she slept a lot. She'd had a rough night already, so he didn't bother to call her. If she was asleep, she needed the rest. Their baby would arrive soon, and she'd need all of her energy for that.

Rager spoke with the soldier at the door as he landed and felt assured that all was well. There were soldiers placed all around the property, at all of the doors and windows, it would be impossible for anything to happen to Ann, even in her vulnerable state.

He took off his armor in his office and then headed into the kitchen. He was thirsty, but not hungry, and drank down almost an entire jug of the stuff Ann called orange juice. It wasn't bad and soothed the thirst he had built up. The armor was great at protecting him, but it didn't always keep him from sweating.

With his thirst satisfied, Rager carefully walked up the stairs. He knew the marble stairs didn't make a sound, but his feet might. He wanted to see Ann, to assure himself she was just fine, because something in him had started to become distressed. Something deep, that he'd only felt once before.

When Ann was taken. The feeling blossomed into something more, primal fear, and he ran up the last few stairs, and down the hall to their room, he threw open the door, and found Katy on the floor, barking her tiny little head off at the open doors to the veranda. Rager flicked on the light and found the bed empty, with no trace of Ann.

He glanced in the bathroom just in case, then ran out of the doors, Katy yapping on his heels. He couldn't see anything, anyone, not even Ann. She wasn't there, she'd simply vanished. He had no direction to run in, nowhere to look. With a roar of rage, he ran back into the house and down the stairs.

"My mate, my mate is gone! Find her! Now!"

Soldiers scrambled, voices started to call out around the perimeters, but nobody had seen anything. Ann, for all that he could tell, had simply vanished.

Rager knew that wasn't the case though. Rex had her. He'd taken her, somehow, and this time, Rager wouldn't just let him slip away. He'd hunt the bastard down himself and strangle him with his bare hands.

Rager went to the transporter and back to the mothership. Katy was left in the care of one of his female soldiers and would be taken care of. For now, he had to focus on his mate, and try to find her.

"Track her," he said once he was on the ship, and he didn't have to say who to track or who was meant to track her. The computer knew from the tone of his voice, another program designed to interpret the emotion expressed in a person's voice, that Rager was in distress and that only one person could cause that kind of distress.

"Tracking now, Overlord," the computer said, her tone even, placid, to soothe him.

Rager gathered a range of new weapons and went back to the transporter. By the time the computer had located his mate and gave him the direction she was headed, Rager was calm, cold, and collected.

He wouldn't escape this time. Rager would hunt him down with his last breath. This time. Rex would not escape with his life. He was too much of a threat to Ann.

Rager could understand the younger man's fascination with Ann, she was all that was good and hopeful in the world. But Rager knew it wasn't those qualities Rex found so attractive about Ann. No, he knew the man was attracted to Ann because he wanted to destroy those qualities, Rex was a very sick man.

The computer had picked up on it when he was first brought in. At the time, it was considered an anomaly, a quirk of the man being a shifter. He was obsessed with Ann, even then, but it was a sick obsession, one that was ugly and full of hate. It was one of the reasons he'd been put into service as a gardener. It would keep him away from Ann but would allow him to be near his family.

Not many of the humans had families left, so to have two families that knew each other was all but impossible. It was decided that they'd be kept together, but Rex had caused some concern. Rager had agreed with the computer, at the time, and thought that the problem would be resolved over time.

Instead, it seemed to have increased. Rex had put other people in danger, not once but twice, so that he could kidnap Ann. This was abhorrent behavior, and this time, it would cost him his life.

"Overlord, I'm sorry to interrupt, but the signal from your mate has disappeared. Her captor must have destroyed it."

"Does Target One have one in still?" Rager hoped it would be the case, but the computer quickly dashed that hope.

"No, Overlord."

"Fuck!" Rager's fist struck the panel of the transporter and he brought it to a stop. He had no idea where they were headed or how to track her down now.

For the first time in his life, Rager felt completely helpless and without a direction to go in, he felt powerless. He sat back in his seat and looked down at the scene below. He'd hadn't quite realized it, but he'd been following a road. A road that ran all the way up California. He could follow it for a while, see if he overtook them before they turned off. That was the only hope he had right now that he'd get his mate back before Rex did something to harm her.

16

There was a sound, a sensation that was oddly also a sound. A vibration maybe? Why was the bed so hard? Was that metal? Was she in a truck bed? How?

Ann knew before she opened her eyes that she wasn't in her bed. She wasn't sure how that had happened, but for the moment, it didn't matter. Her brain was fuzzy, her head hurt, and her body ached. Where was she?

Fear started to trickle in when she opened her eyes and saw the panel of a truck bed, as she suspected. It sped down the road, and the frigidly cold wind blew over her prone body with a cruel touch. She pulled her legs up, to try to sit up, but it wasn't easy to do. The truck kept swerving around and the momentum would knock her over.

She finally rolled to her side and pushed her way around. She was clumsier than she usually was, and her body didn't exactly want to cooperate. That was more than just her pregnancy and she began to wonder if she'd been drugged. And if she'd been drugged that could only mean one thing.

Rex.

She pushed herself up against the place where the wheel made an arch in the bed. She could make out the back of someone's head, and when she tilted her head a little more, she could make out the face.

"Shit! Rex! You fucking termite! Let me out of this thing!" She managed to throw herself against the glass at the back of the cab and beat against it. "Let me out of this truck, you putrid little bastard!"

He jerked and swerved when he heard her and then saw she was about to put her fists through the glass. He lifted a rather evil looking pistol and pointed it at her as he stomped on the brake.

"Stop that, or I will shoot you and get this all over with." He shouted it at her through the glass.

As usual, Rex had been stupid and hadn't thought things through.

The gun made her pause, but he hadn't tied her hands or her feet together, the stupid fucking idiot, so she moved to the back of the truck and decided to wait.

The gun didn't scare her,. He obviously wanted her alive or he'd have killed her already. She smirked at him as he turned back around.

She'd just jump out of the truck when he stopped the next time.

She hadn't counted on how cold it was though. Or the fact that all she had on was a pair of gray jogging pants and another black hoodie. She'd freeze before he stopped again.

She didn't even have socks on, so she pulled the bottoms of her pants down to cover them. She'd be frozen by the time he stopped, if he stopped before she actually died. What was he up to this time?

Well, it was obvious what he was up to, she thought, but why? Why again? Some hatred he had of Rager? Or did he think this was payback for escaping him the first time? And leaving him, her mind added.

That was probably it. She'd left him and that was just too much for his brain to take. The fact that he'd made it back was a show of just how deep his hatred ran. It must have been a nightmare to try to get back to their sector.

She thought about Amanda for a moment, how sad the woman had been since Rex had disappeared into the wilds on the other side of the rift. She'd got on with life, but there was a sadness about her that nothing could take away. This would only deepen that sadness. Ann had come to realize, as her baby grew inside of her, that as a mother, Amanda must be sad for her child.

It would break her own heart if this baby grew up to be a monster like Rex. Even if he wasn't very good at being a monster. He'd partially succeed then mess it up somehow. And maybe that was even worse for Amanda. Because those mistakes might be signs that he wasn't that bad. That he wasn't that evil.

And she wouldn't have to question why her son was so bad, then either. Even though Ann was certain she did. It was a complex situation, made worse because Amanda knew Ann, had known Ann most of her life.

Ann grimaced as the truck bounced and she landed on something sharp. It was a tire iron, with a sharp end, a good weapon, but not a good idea to leave floating around the back of a truck. It barely broke her skin, but it was enough to make her bleed. She could feel the blood that ran down her back, but she couldn't really see the wound. She kicked at the back of the cab until Rex raised the pistol again. Fuckwit.

She moved, huddled up against the cab where the wind most passed her by, and tried to figure out what to do. She couldn't run, her belly was far too heavy for that, but she could waddle quickly. Could she waddle fast enough though?

Exhaustion began to pull at her as the road noise made by the tires lulled her. She slept a lot lately, quite a lot. Would she be able to stay awake long enough to get away from him? What if she fell asleep, he stopped, and she didn't know it? She tried to stay awake, tried to fight the sleep that pulled at her eyes, but she couldn't.

She felt the bumps when Rex hit something, he probably should have avoided it, and felt the truck begin to climb a hill. Every bump woke her up just a little bit, and the climb up the hill caused her to slide down to the tailgate. That woke her up more fully than the bumps did because, for a moment, she was afraid she would fall out of the truck.

She came fully awake when Rex pulled off the road and onto a track that was now overgrown with thin trees and grass. Her heart thudded in her chest as she saw where they were. He was headed right for the bunker they'd hid in for all those years. He could keep her there for the rest of her life, if he managed to shut that hatch with her inside. She clutched at the tire iron and tried to calm her breath down.

When he pulled to a stop in front of the small shack that led to the hatch, Ann tried to get over the tailgate, but he got out of the truck and ran to stop her. The gun in her back soon calmed her down.

"Don't fight me, Ann. That's done. You're going down into that bunker and that's all there is to it."

"I will not!" she refuted and spat at him, but he just

slapped her, hard enough to make her ears ring, and growled at her.

"I'm done playing with you, Ann. Do it now or I'll beat you to death and leave your body up here to rot." The coldness in his eyes told her that the old Rex was gone, and this was someone new. Someone that had survived, learned to kill, and would do it again in an instant.

Oh fuck, she thought, and turned to go into the shack.

She pulled open the round hatch and climbed into the chute that led down to the bunker. There was a pain between her shoulder blades, a pain that made her wince, and she wondered what it was. It dawned on her when her fingers slipped the first time and the sudden move made the painful spot sting even more, that it was the spot where her tracker had been. Rex must have removed it.

She knew she had to keep moving though so she did the only thing she could do and continued the climb down. It took her some time; the chute was narrow, and the rungs built into the cement walls were thin. Her fingers kept slipping, because her palms were moist with fear, and she was terrified she'd fall. She finally made it down to the ground and tried to waddle away from him.

She could lock herself up in the food storage area,

and that would be the end of it. He'd starve to death after a while, and she could get out. But she couldn't move fast enough. Rex caught up to her and pushed her in the direction of her old quarters.

"Fuck off in there, and don't come out unless I tell you to." Rex waited for her to shut the door and then pushed a metal bar through the slots on each side of the door.

She hadn't noticed the slots when she'd lived there in the past, so he must have come here and installed the slots before he came for her. She stared out through the thick window in the door at the man that had just locked her in. He was more rugged, dirty, and now looked like the insane man she knew him to be.

He was talking to himself about something, but she couldn't hear what it was he said. She watched him for a while, tried to plead with him to let her go, but he ignored her or didn't hear her. He walked off, in the direction of the food storage area, and she finally decided to stop her vigil.

Rex would not let her out, and she knew that if Rager didn't find her somehow, that she would die here. Rex didn't seem to care whether she was alive or not, he just wanted her there for some reason she couldn't fathom. Revenge was the highest on her list of guesses.

She'd counted on his stupidity the first time he'd kidnapped her. He wasn't so naïve this time, and he'd obviously done a lot of planning. How he'd gotten into the house was beyond her. He must have drugged her somehow, and carried her out, but how he'd gotten past the guards was another mystery. One she doubted she'd ever get an answer to.

Then there was the truck. Most vehicles wouldn't work now for quite a few reasons. The batteries were dead was the first problem. Then there was the fact that valves, hoses, and seals became thin with the cold, cracked over time, and became little more than dust as time wore on. A car's engine was full of rubber and plastic that broke down with the cold temperatures. All of that would have to be replaced with new ones, and finding parts that hadn't become useless, even in the deserted auto parts stores, was rare.

Then came the final problem. Cars needed fuel to run in the engine, if the person managed to replace all the parts that were damaged. Ann knew people could make a kind of diesel from old cooking oil, but that took time and wasn't very good for engines. Alcohol made from corn would work too, but she thought that required replacing some parts of an engine. She'd read about it all in a book she'd found down here all those years ago.

Somehow, he'd managed it, because the truck ran without a hitch, and he'd brought them there. Now, the question was, what did he want with her? He'd threatened to kill her baby the last time he had her. Ann's hands clutched at her stomach and she stared at the window. She still had the tire iron, stuck down in her underwear at her hip. She took it out, hid it under her bed, and decided she'd just have to wait and see what happened.

There was nothing she could do now but wait.

* * *

SOMETHING WAS WRONG. She could feel it. Rex had left her alone for three days. He'd slid food in through a slot she hadn't noticed in the door and dropped in bottles of water, but he hadn't let her out of the quarters she was in. Luckily, there was a toilet and a shower in there, although, as she became ill, she needed to pee less than she normally did. All she'd used the toilet for today was the sporadic vomiting that kept hitting her.

The problem seemed to be the wound in her back, the one from the tire iron. It was infected, and now it had started to smell a bit on top of the intense pain it caused her. The other wound seemed to be infected too, but not as badly. She was certain that she was very ill, from either one or both. She needed a doctor, and Rex didn't care.

She'd cleaned the bottom wound as best she could but without antibiotic ointment or proper care, it had become infected. Now, she suspected it was worse than a simple infection. She had a fever, she was nauseous and vomiting, and her pulse was high. She knew they were all symptoms of septicemia, and without help, she would die.

"Rex!" she called when she heard his footsteps. She was so ill she could barely move, but she used the strength she had to call out to him. "Rex, I need help!"

But he didn't walk to her door, and the sound of her pitiful cries was all that broke the silence. She would die here, alone, uncared for, with her baby inside her, unborn. She tried to think of something, anything that she could use to cut herself open before she died, but there was nothing sharp enough in the room.

If she could find something she'd use it to break her water, force the delivery of her baby, but what would happen then? Rex had turned into a cold, unfeeling monster. He would just leave her baby there to die. Maybe it was best that the baby died along with her. He might do something worse with the baby, if she had it.

She was feverish, perhaps delirious, so she might be crazy, but she thought that might really be for the best. That way, he couldn't hurt her baby, or torture it. Sweat broke out on her skin as she began to shiver. He wouldn't touch her baby, not if she could help it. She pulled the blanket up over her head and turned to face the wall, even though it increased her nausea to move and made the pain in her back almost unbearable.

She wouldn't even look at him. She'd just lie there, and hopefully die before he could do anything worse to her.

$\mathcal{A}$ strange calm settled over Rager. He'd been frantic for the last three days, uncertain and frustrated as he tried to figure out where his mate was. He'd gone through stages. The first day he'd followed the road that she'd been on until he fell asleep. When he woke up, the transporter had stopped moving.

He'd gone back to the mothership and tried to use the computer to find her, but nothing had worked. The second day, he and his soldiers combed side streets, paths, anything that might even remotely look like a road. By that evening, he had a burning pain in his back that would not leave him alone.

He finally woke up on the third day, sick with worry. Literally. He'd tossed up his breakfast and hadn't even bothered with lunch. That didn't stop him from searching though. He'd run out of places to look, so he went to Ann's father.

"Are you certain Rex has her?" John asked, his face just as worried as Rager's. He was Ann's father, of course he was worried sick, too, Rager thought. Maybe even more so than Rager.

"I am." Rager looked around, but didn't see a familiar face in the living room. "Where's Mary? With the babies?"

"Yes, but she's heartbroken about Ann. She won't leave the babies now, not unless it's to go to Ann. I'm really worried about her, but there's nothing I can do. I've thought about…" his words trailed off and he shook his head.

"You've thought about what?" Rager prodded, curious to know what his thoughts were. John was an intelligent man, one of the most intelligent that Rager had made a mayor. He respected the man, not just because he was Ann's father, but because of how he governed and always had his hand in things. He didn't just sit back and make decrees like some minor king, he actually took part in the business of governing, and that impressed Rager.

"I've thought about taking Mary and the babies back into the bunker, at least until we found out what's happened to Ann. I think Mary would feel so much better there, more secure you know."

"But you took all the food out, didn't you?" Rager thought that's what had happened anyway.

"Not all of it." He looked a little guilty, then brought his head up, just a little defiant. "We weren't sure how things would go here, so we left some. Just in case."

"Smart man." Rager nodded and smiled with a hint of pride. "You are a good and smart man, John."

"I hope so. I only want what's best for my wife and children. All of them." He sighed and looked at Rager. "I had another thought; one I hope I'm wrong about."

"What's that?" Rager leaned forward on the couch, his hands together at his knees.

"If Rex took her, he might have taken her to the bunker. You haven't been there, have you?"

"No, I haven't been there. But it's a place to look. Somewhere that's familiar to him, and out of the way." John's eyes were lined, dark, but now bright with hope,

"And off the road that Ann was last tracked on." Rager was already counting out how many soldiers he'd have to take with him.

"Yes. I guess he thought about it at some point on the way up there, stopped, and took her tracker out. And his." John couldn't seem to think of a better explanation of why Ann's tracker stopped working.

"I almost wish we hadn't moved them to the back now, Ann might have been able to fool him into thinking she had it removed. Everyone knows that's where we put them now, not on the arm."

"It's not your fault. Rex is sick, mentally. He's no good for anybody now."

"I'll deal with him, don't worry. And I'll try not to kill him." Rager didn't want to make the promise but felt he should. Since he'd made it, he knew he'd try to keep it.

"That might be best for Amanda and her husband. They're done with him, I think, but if he was dead, it might be worse."

"We can't have him on this planet anymore. If I do capture him, he'll be sent to another planet. You realize that, don't you?" The hard look on his face said death might be a better option.

"Alive is better than dead. Unless Ann is," he paused, caught his breath and blinked rapidly, his emotions getting the better of him, "unless Ann is dead. Then, I don't care what happens to him."

"I understand." Rager knew that Rex would die if Ann wasn't breathing. That would end all promises he'd made up to this point.

"I'll draw you a map, in fact, I'll come with you. And call Skye, Ann may need her."

"Skye may still be in the clinic. I'll call and see if she's well. If not, I'll get Meg to come with us." Rager didn't want to think about John's last words. Ann may need her.

There could be a thousand reasons why Ann might need Skye. It didn't have to mean anything… bad. But in the back of his mind, Rager knew anything was possible. Rex had completely lost it, if he was the reason Ann was gone. That still hadn't been confirmed.

He hadn't been found in the sector, obviously, but he had been seen. Now he was gone, and so was Ann. It was easy to put the two together. Rager could only hope it was the right assumption to make.

"I'll get some soldiers down here," Rager said and went outside to wait after he made the calls.

There was an oppressive air in the house, as if the people inside already mourned the child they had lost. Rager hoped he'd brought a spark of hope back to the place, but it wasn't enough. Not yet. Not until Ann was back home.

John followed him out and spoke as they waited. "In the old world, people went missing all the time. We blamed you guys. Well, little green versions of you guys."

"Not a bad theory." Rager had to agree.

"No. But most of the time, it was just a matter of people didn't want to think about the truth. Children, adults, all were slaughtered by the hands of other people. Most of the time the people were sick, mentally, you know? The kind of sick that made them do really bad things. We hoped that wouldn't bleed over to this new world you all made for us. Now, well, Mary's up there, in that room of hers, holed up with the babies, because the truth is, that sickness did follow us to this world. It's not your fault," John quickly amended, "it's not something you can do anything about. It's something in us, evil some people like to call it."

"I understand." Rager nodded. "My own world hasn't found a cure for that either."

"It's in you guys too, then?" John asked, his face down, his shoulders slumped.

"I think it's in all life, even in the animal world. It's not something we can stop, it would seem," Rager responded, his eyes on the horizon, waiting for that transporter that would bring his soldiers.

"No. It doesn't seem we can. Except isolate it and keep it away from the rest of the world."

"When it's as bad as this, yes. It has to be isolated, dealt with, by whatever means necessary."

"You're right."

The two men stepped down from the steps as the transporter came down to the ground. They both got into Rager's transporter and John sat down in the passenger seat. Rager took the driver's seat, and they headed out, both full of hope that this would be the last time they'd have to go out.

It took a while, longer than Rager remembered, but they made it back to the remains of the highway that headed in the direction of the bunker. He became nauseous about an hour after they started, but he pushed it down. The sensation became stronger the longer he drove, and John took over.

"I think it's her. This feels strange, like it's someone's sickness, not mine. But I can feel it." He pushed his head down between his knees, and breathed in deeply, gently.

"She's ill then," John surmised. "Skye is with your troops, right?"

"Yeah, she's recovered enough, so she came with them."

"Good," Ann's father said, and steered the transporter off the road. "It's up this hill, and then there should be a little shack. The entrance is in there."

"Alright. Set it down. Is that your vehicle there?" Rager asked when the truck came into view.

"No, ours is that old SUV over there. I don't know who that truck belongs to."

"Someone's here then. Set it down."

John did as instructed and then put on some armor that one of the soldiers handed to him once they made it outside.

"You stay at the back, until it's clear, understand?" Rager barked at John, already in battle mode.

"Yes, I do." John nodded, the helmet bobbed on his head in a way that almost made Rager laugh, but he just gave a curt nod instead.

"Let's go." Two of the soldiers moved in, set some

explosives on the hatch when they determined it would open, and came out.

A moment later the shack blew apart and the hatch was open.

"Come down here, you alien scum. Let me show you what I've got for you." Yes, that was definitely Rex's voice, Rager thought.

"Send the drone down," he ordered, and the soldiers went to the hatch, a small drone in one's hands. The other one took a set of controls from a patch on their pant leg and began to move the droid down into the hatch. A screen appeared, and they could all see Rex stood there, a psychotic grin on his face as he stared down the barrel of a rifle at the droid.

"Tag him," Rager ordered and Rex fell. He knew the droid had sent out a tranquilizer. "Let me in."

Rager quickly made his way down the rungs and looked around. He couldn't see Ann or anyone else for that matter.

He saw a few doors and went to them as the other soldiers came down. Rex was knocked out on the floor, and Rager didn't miss the not so gentle kick John gave him before he rushed to one door in particular. Rager could see there was a bar blocking that door.

"Bring Skye down!" Rager called out and rushed to push the bar off the door for John.

"Ann!" his mate's father cried and ran into the room.

There was a woman, large with child, on the bed, but she didn't respond. Rager knew it was his mate, he could feel her now, the fever that raged in her system, and it nearly knocked him to his knees. He had to steady himself and leaned into the wall as Skye rushed in, medical kit in hand.

She took one look at Ann and turned to Rager. "We need a hospital. Now. And Meg too. I don't know that I can do this on my own."

"We've brought some of our medical robots. Let's get her out of here and in a hospital. Even dusty will be better than this place," Rager said and went to pick up his mate to carry her up.

"Take him to the mothership and lock him in one of the high-security cages." Rager gave Rex his own kick as he walked by him. Then he walked back and kicked him again. It wasn't as satisfying as a punch to the head, but the man was passed out.

He carried Ann up and sat her down on the seat. John stood behind Rager and guided him in the direction of the hospital. Skye was in the other transporter with some soldiers. The others would wait for a new transporter. They had orders to kill Rex if he so much as looked like he thought about escaping. He was not to make it out of their sight.

Ann was in bad shape, and Rager wanted nothing more than to hold her, but he could feel how sick she was. He could tell they were running out of time. Just hold on, he whispered to himself, over and over.

It took twenty minutes, but they finally found a hospital and landed on the top of the building. Rager picked her up, carried her out, and they ran through the door his soldier kicked open. They ran down dark halls until they found the labor ward.

"Down here," the soldier called, and they all followed her. Another soldier had one robot in hand, while the other carried a box that contained the larger one.

Rager followed along, with John behind them, until they came to a room that looked right. Skye was right, it was dusty, but it was good enough for now. He put Ann down on the bed, just as she scrunched up. He thought she was awake, but he could see she wasn't.

"I need power in here. Who can get me that?" Skye looked at Rager, and he nodded at a soldier bringing lines down from the transporters. "He can, plug whatever you need into that. The transporter can handle it.

"Awesome," Skye said and went to wash her hands. "Get her clothes off and let's have a look at her."

Rager began to undress his mate and took the blanket a soldier found in a cupboard. There were people everywhere, but somehow it was all still orderly and ran without a hitch. Good training, he supposed.

"She's in labor, I think," Skye said from her place beside Ann. "Her clothes were soaked, and I can feel her pulling into herself, even though she's unconscious. Her body is working to do what it needs to do. But right now, from the smell of her, it's the last thing she needs to do."

"Deploy that small robot. It will start to administer whatever she needs." If it's not too late were words he refused to say. He could feel she was close to death, and he used every ounce of will he had to reach out to her, to bring her back to the land of the living.

The soldier set the smallest of the two robots on a table beside Ann and an arm came out. It scanned her entire body, then administered two injections.

"Pain medicine and something that must be an antibiotic?" Skye looked at Rager for confirmation.

"Looks like it." He frowned, then spoke. "Let's clean her up, find out what her injuries are."

Rager hadn't seen it when he undressed her, he'd been too busy protecting her from the view of the soldiers, but the second he turned her over to swipe at her back with a cloth doused in alcohol, he saw the angry red and black wound in her back. "Fuck, Skye, look at this!"

"Fucking hell. I need to clean that, maybe even remove some of the skin. I need scalpels, people. Look in the drawers, see what you can find."

The small robot moved back into life, and a new arm came out, this one with a scalpel in hand. The first arm came out with a small nozzle on the end, and the wound was washed, dead skin cut away, then filled with an ointment that Rager knew would start to work immediately. Still, Ann was just out of reach, but the fever started to slowly fade. He didn't feel so hot, or ill.

Then the robot pushed Ann further onto her side, and the saw the other wound. It was deeper, and went straight into her spine, from the looks of it. They might be too late, that wound said. The infection might be too deep to save her.

18

She could feel Rager now. For so long he felt as if he was far away, but now, she felt him near her. He gave her strength, though it felt like a futile effort. She was so far gone, she and the baby.

She felt pain like it was a flare that remained after a bright flash. The linger of odd shadows, once the light is gone. It was there, she knew she felt it, but it was distanced from her. She felt the fever though, it raged around her, this fire that burned in cycle, over and over, without end.

She thought she heard the baby, a small voice, a cry, but she wasn't sure. Maybe she was only delirious, maybe this wasn't real. Maybe she was dead already and didn't know.

"Stay with me, Ann. Don't leave me."

She could hear Rager's voice, and she tried to open

her eyes, but her eyelids felt as if they'd been taped down. She tried to lift her hand, to reach for him, but something held it down. Or so it felt like.

Ann distanced herself from it all, drew back into the darkness, where the pain didn't nag at her, where the fire didn't burn so hot through her body and brain.

"She's not responding."

Skye's voice drew her out of the darkness, but even that couldn't keep her fully awake.

"Are there more powerful drugs?" she heard Skye ask.

"The robot will give her what she needs."

Ann drew back as the fire came again, melting away her resistance to the darkness. She wanted to wake up, to be a part of the world again, but the fire hurt so much.

"It's cleaning the wound in her back, that one I think goes right into her spine."

"That can't be good," Ann tried to say, but her lips wouldn't move. She realized she'd responded to Skye's voice, but again, the darkness called to her.

A pain pierced through even the numbing darkness, a pain that felt like a needle had just punctured her spinal cord, and in the darkness she screamed. It was loud, it rang around the empty space, and came back at her, just as pain gripped her down below. Pain that felt as if it wanted to rip her hips apart and leave her split right up the middle.

Ann clutched at... nothing. There was nothing to hold onto, nothing to push against as pain and fire consumed her. This was not supposed to happen. This was not what she wanted. She wanted her mate, her baby, her parents. Her mom.

"Momma!" she called the word out into the darkness as the pain in her lower abdomen subsided. "Momma, I can't do this alone!"

But her mother wasn't there.

"I'm here, Ann, I won't leave you, sweetheart." Rager's voice again, his finger on her cheek to dry the tear she didn't know had fallen. "Come back to us, baby, please."

"Her blood pressure is too high, I think she's diving into eclampsia."

"What does that mean?"

"The baby will have to come out. Can the robot do surgery?"

Ann wanted to scream, to tell them to wait, she could do this, but she couldn't even wake up, so how could she give birth to her baby? She'd wanted to go through the whole experience, to feel it all, after she'd watched her mother do it.

"Fuck, it's too high! Get that machine ready now!" Skye shouted at someone, and Ann felt the pressure of a cuff around her arm. She heard the beep as the machines measured her heart rate, her blood pressure, and oxygen levels. "Somebody get Meg here now!"

Ann could hear the panic in Skye's voice, she wanted to tell her to stay calm, it would be alright, but the darkness called just as the pain began again, and then the fire swarmed back into life.

Ann retreated, far away, to escape the agony that invaded her, that pervaded her body. She retreated back into the past, to a time when she had best friends, and a crush on the hottie next door, to a time when her Mom was her main best friend, above everyone else.

"What are you reading?" Ann asked her mother, who was curled up in the window seat of their house. Sunlight turned her hair into a halo that dazzled Ann. She'd always wanted her mother's beautiful blond hair, but she had her father's dark hair instead.

"A romance novel, my love. Something light and fun. What do you have?"

Ann looked down at the book, unsure all of a sudden. "Oh, it's a horror novel. Something I found in the school library. Teenaged werewolves and vampires, you know?"

"We all need our escapes, don't we dear. Come up here and sit with me." Mary moved over and Ann, barely 13, moved to snuggle at her mom's side. "Shall we go to the movies later? It's Saturday, and you know what that means."

"We can do whatever we want." Ann grinned. She didn't care what they did, she just liked to spend time with her mom.

"Want to invite your friends?" Mary asked, and tilted her head. Ann noticed there were flames in her eyes but ignored the twin flares of orange. It wasn't weird at all that orange had appeared in those light blue eyes.

"No, just us tonight, I think. And Dad if he wants to come."

"I think he'll be at work, but we can go by ourselves. We'll see that new romantic comedy. The one with that actor you like so much."

"Evan Andrews. He's so gorgeous!" Ann giggled and her mom tickled her abdomen. The tickle became painful for a moment, but Ann frowned and moved away.

"Sorry, honey. Why don't you go change and I'll get ready too? We can go eat after we go to the pool."

"Sure," Ann said without even blinking over the mention of the pool. It all made sense here, even when it didn't.

It was better than that other world. Ann screamed as fire burned her all over again, and then pushed it back, drew even further back into herself, into the darkness. There was no Mom here, no Dad, and definitely no Rager.

This was a cold world, an ice age of mammoths and

bears so large they could kill a man with the swipe of a paw. She was cold, naked, and people stood on a hill to look at her. She pulled her arms around herself, to hide her nudity, to try and ward off the cold. It didn't work, it was still cold.

"Help me!" she called to the people on the hill, but they left her. Turned away, wrapped in their furs and leather, and left her.

She was naked, alone, in the cold and snow. She tried to move, to find somewhere to hide, but the skin of her feet was frozen to the ground. She looked down in horror and screamed all over again. Her feet were fused to the ground!

"Help me! Rager, please! Get me out of here!" Her brain screamed the words, but he wasn't there, not in that cold place.

She could see, in the distance, an orange glow that reminded her of just how cold she was. She sank to the ground, unable to move, unable to fight her way out of this place.

"Momma," she muttered again, and in an instant, she was back in the living room, cradled in her mother's arm in the window seat.

"What movie do you want to see?"

Ann looked at her mother and thought. She'd already forgotten she'd answered the question.

A feeling took over, a sensation of being pulled down

a drain as she sank into herself, made her close her eyes. Then pain ripped her apart.

"Rager!" she screamed his name as she came back to life, fully back to life, if for only a moment. There were bright lights and darkness. Faces that she couldn't make out stared down at her, and she was in an unfamiliar place. Where was she? What was happening? "Rager?"

The name came out pitifully, full of the fear and anxiety she felt.

"I'm here, honey. Skye's here, and Meg. They're doing their best, Ann. Stay with us baby." He looked down at her, his orange eyes aflame as he smiled. "Don't go, Ann, please don't go."

But a searing pain across her lower abdomen spun her back into the darkness, away from the light, away from the face she adored the most. His face.

She didn't go so far away this time. She drifted in the darkness, able to hear the people in the real world, but not able to respond.

"Her blood pressure is rising again." Skye's voice drifted away, and Ann fell into soft nothingness.

She wasn't aware of anything, and finally the pain was gone. Voices were a background noise as she walked in her garden, at her home with Rager, a place where she felt at peace and quiet. The noise was gone, as was the pain, the deep burn that came with the flames, and the fear. She heard a baby cry, and turned to see her child, in a crib, over by a tall rose bush.

She went to the baby and looked down. The child with a light fuzz of dark hair, smiled up at her, happy as it stretched in the crib. It was dressed all in white, and for a moment, she was confused because she didn't know its gender or name. She was the child's mother, surely she should know?

But it didn't matter, she decided, and she picked the baby up. The little eyes opened, a blaze of orange fire that brought a smile to Ann's face. It had its father's eyes, at least. The child looked like her, though, it had the tilted corners of her eyelids, her nose, and the shape of her face.

Baby's sometimes looked bland, like they could belong to anyone with flat, round features that didn't stand out. This child's face looked just like hers, and she knew that this was the baby she'd waited so long for. She walked with the baby, and soon, Katy was on her heels, with a rambunctious yip and jump to say hello.

Heaven, if only Rager were here. She walked around, dressed in a long white gown that reminded her of the way women dressed in the early 1900s. She even had on one of those silly huge white hats, with feathers sticking down one side. She didn't care though, this was better than where she'd been… before.

For a moment, the frantic sound of beeps far too

close together broke into her peaceful world, but a soldier, dressed in white, came and the beeps disappeared. She was safe now, there were soldiers near.

The world started to fade after a time. The baby disappeared from her arms, a new pain sliced into her, from her back this time, and people began to shout.

"She's losing too much blood." A voice that sounded like Meg mumbled.

Who was losing too much blood?

"It's there, a nicked vessel," Skye said, and Ann suddenly felt a faint burn.

"The baby isn't responding." A voice she didn't know spoke from somewhere, and Ann tried to turn her head, but she couldn't.

"Get the robot on it." Rager, he was there! She knew he wouldn't leave her!

"We're losing her."

Which her? Her? The baby?

Ann wanted to stay, to find out what was going on. But the darkness pulled at her. She wanted to stay there. Rex wasn't there, this dream wasn't there. The pain, the fire, the anguish wasn't there either. Kind of. It was dulled, not as blunt.

A long beep, that did not stop broke into the fuzziness as Ann drifted away, to a place where sound did not exist as sound. Just as an impression.

"She's crashed. What do we do?" Meg this time.

"Leave the robot to handle it. Just save her, whatever you do." There was a ragged tone in his voice, a sound of unbearable pain, but Ann barely heard it. She was headed back to her garden, where none of this existed.

Warmth came now, but then…

"Ann, don't you dare leave me. Not when I've only just found you. Not now that I love you. Please, Ann, don't leave me."

She heard him, felt the way he kissed her forehead as something wet fell there. Why did he sound so miserable? She was only going to take a nap. To wait for the pain to be gone. She reached for him, tried to pull him with her. But she couldn't, she couldn't reach him, couldn't bring him into this world with her.

There was no sound now. No light. She looked around, tried to find a light, a place to hide or to wander in. The place with her mother maybe. Or the garden. The garden was nice. Ann quickly found, however, that no matter which direction she moved in, there was no light. Even when she tried to move up or down, nothing appeared.

There were no memories here, no sensation. No fire, no pain, no sadness. It was blank. No matter how far out she traveled, or how high, she could not find an end to this black void she found herself in. She concentrated, tried to think of something, anything that might conjure up an image, but all she could remember was right now. Nothing more.

She couldn't remember a face, not even her own, or a voice. She couldn't remember a moment. And now, so many moments after she came here, she couldn't even remember her name. Her knowledge narrowed down to a pinpoint of knowledge. She was here. This place. This moment. This now.

Nothing existed here. Nothing at all. Not even her.

19

"**S**he's awake!" Rager's voice filled the small room, and Ann groaned. Her head hurt and her body felt as if it was weighed down with stones.

"Rager?" she whispered. Why was her throat so dry?

"I'm here, Ann. We're all here." She turned her head, followed the sound of his voice, and opened her eyes.

He was there, with a baby in his arms, wrapped in one of the baby blankets she'd made. "Which one is that?"

"Pardon?" His brows scrunched up together and he gave her a funny look. Then his face cleared as he realized. "You don't know! This is our baby, Ann, not your mother's."

"What? How?" She couldn't remember anything, except going to bed, Katy at the side of the bed, where she'd refused to budge from.

"We got you back from Rex. You were sick, very sick. Your heart even stopped at one point. There was so much wrong…" Rager's voice trailed off and his head tilted down to look at the baby. "Skye did surgery, with the help of the robots, and delivered her. Then, they worked on you. It's been four days."

"Rex took me?" She sat up, now that her head didn't hurt so much, and noticed she had an IV in her arm. "I don't remember anything."

"That's probably for the best," Mary said as she came in, a huge smile on her face. "That boy, always causing trouble. I'm so happy to see you, baby. It's been the worst week of my life!"

Mary hugged her daughter awkwardly, and then her father came in, and more people, and then they all explained exactly what had happened, and all Ann could do was stare at them. That was her baby Rager held? She wanted to hold her. Touch her. Look at her! But Rager just stood there, the baby snug in his arms.

"I love you all, I really do, but have none of you realized yet that I still haven't seen my baby?" She looked at them all, unsure of what else to say to make them understand.

"Fuck, sorry. Yes, here, take her." Rager moved to stand closer to her and gently handed the baby over.

Ann looked down at the baby, and couldn't believe just how much the tiny girl looked like her. She yawned and stretched, opened her eyes, and Ann could have sworn the tiny tot with orange eyes like her father winked at her! She smiled, touched the baby's chin with a fingertip and looked around at the others.

"She's so perfect." Everybody laughed at that, and most filed out with a promise to come back later when she'd had time to get to know her daughter.

Mary and John stayed, along with Rager, in chairs to the left side of Ann's bed.

"You've been through a lot, Ann. We're here to help you, so don't feel overwhelmed, alright?" Mary promised and tried to hide the fact that she wanted to say so much more. "I'm just glad you're awake."

"So, Rex took me again? And I became sick? Then what?"

"Rager found you," John said, "well, he and I found you. You had wounds in your back, one was where he removed your tracker with what must have been a very dirty knife. You had another one, down near your hip, and that was infected too. You also developed preeclampsia, and well, you were very ill when we found you, honey."

"Your heart stopped at one point, the trauma just became too much. You had so much going on." Ann could tell by the pain that flitted across his face that he was reliving those moments. "You were leaving us, but somehow you fought your way back. Skye and Meg did all that they could, but you had to choose it seems. Your heart had stopped, they couldn't get it started."

His voice broke off and Mary took over. "That was the point when I arrived. Your dad and Rager were both just… devastated, and I walked in. They said you were gone, but I didn't believe them. I couldn't believe them. You're my baby. So, I took your hand and watched while Skye and Meg worked on your little girl, and well, that was when your heart came back to life. There was this tiny bleep, and a few seconds later, another, then, it came back at a normal pace."

"It was unbelievable. I've never seen anything like it." Rager sounded as if he was still stunned by the whole thing.

"A mother's love. That's all it took." Ann held her hand out to her Mom with a pleased smile. "Thank you, Mom."

"Well, you just give all of that same love to this little girl, won't you? She'll need it I think." Mary let go of Ann's hand, and looked at Rager with a glare before she turned back to Ann. "Now, what are you naming her? Rager wouldn't tell us."

"It might sound old fashioned, but her name is Stella. It's Latin for star. Her father came from the stars to save us all and so, I thought it best to give her a name that meant something." Ann looked down at little Stella and felt love unlike anything she'd known before. This was her baby, and she'd die for her.

"It's the perfect name. It means star in our language too." Rager told them and nodded. "It's a good name."

"I'm glad you approve." Ann grinned at him and then winked. She was back to life and had a lot to look forward to. "Um, there are no lasting effects to what happened, right?"

"You'll have some scarring on your back, but only faint scars. The robots did a good job. And Skye and Meg too. Otherwise, you should be fine." Rager assured her with a gentle tone to his voice.

"Good." She scooted down in the bed, her abdomen a little sore, but otherwise, she didn't feel too bad. Even the headache had disappeared. "May I have something to eat and drink then?"

"Of course! I'll go get you something." John jumped up and Mary followed behind, to make sure he could carry everything.

Rager poured her a glass of water, and she drank it while she waited for her parents to come back. "Our little girl, Rager. Are you okay with her being a girl?"

"Why wouldn't I be?" he asked, confused.

"Because she's not a boy. Your world might not have as much gender bias as mine did, but there's still some."

"You're right. I wanted to study, to be a scholar, but my

family insisted I be a warrior instead. They chose to send me off to this planet before I was even old enough to walk. All I wanted to do was read, find new places to study, and learn. I was meant to be their crowning achievement." His face darkened with sadness, and maybe just a little resentment. "Here in this world, I've noticed how men are favored. We appointed men to the highest places, because of that bias. I guess we were wrong to do that."

"I don't want her to grow up in a world where she's a pawn because of the gender she was born into. I don't want her to have to feel like she's second best, or to feel like she can't reach her goals because she's a girl. I've noticed the old ways have crept in, women are losing their status, and we have to stop that." Ann looked at him, a plea in her eyes. "I don't ever want some boy to feel like she owes him something, just because he likes her."

"That's how Rex made you feel," Rager surmised. "And I see your point. He looked at you as his, even though you rejected him, over and over."

"He did, and I don't want Stella to have to deal with that. We can't just teach our girls, and women, that they're equal to men, we have to teach the boys too. It shouldn't even be a question, really. Women shouldn't have to fight to get what they deserve, or to remind men that they're just as worthy of the goals they set as the men are." She frowned, then she smiled an apology. "Sorry, got on my soapbox."

"You stay on that soapbox, Ann. You, of all people, know what it's like to be treated in the worst way by men. Skye does too, I think. So many of you do. It's sad really."

"We can sort it out together, my love." She winced, she hadn't meant to say that last part. "Can we talk about one more thing?"

"What's that?" He scooted close, took her hand, and kissed the top of the baby's head. Ann placed the baby in her lap and looked over at Rager.

"I have to tell you something. Something I've wanted to say for a long time, but, well, life got in the way, it didn't seem right at other times. And, well, I wasn't sure you'd want to hear it. But, we nearly lost the chance to be truly honest with each other, and I don't want to waste any more time on being proper and correct all the time."

"You don't have to be with me, Ann. You've always been exactly what I want you to be. Perfectly you." He kissed the back of her knuckles and waited.

"I love you, Rager. I have loved you for a very long time, and I want to be your partner in everything we do. Not just the little things, the things we do at home, but everything."

"Then you will be, Ann. Where I come from, love is

not a word we use. It's not something I think most of us know, even. We've read about it, but I'm not sure we feel it. Or, I didn't, until you came along. And since the day I met you, well, I've loved you, Ann. That's only grown stronger and clearer to me with every day that's passed. I love you."

Ann felt tears well up in her eyes and tried to blink them away, but they just wouldn't go. He stood up, wiped her face, and bent down to kiss her. "I love you, Ann. You are my mate, my love, and now the mother of my child. From now on, you will not know fear, if I can help it at all. You will know only love, joy, and happiness."

"That's impossible, but I think you'll try your best." Ann couldn't help but laugh at herself, and her tears. "I'll try to do the same."

"Good thing you two are already mated, or I'd tell you to get a room." Skye walked in with a grin on her face, her eyebrows two wiggling black lines across her face. "Give her time to heal, man, before you go trying to make her a mommy again."

"I will." Rager looked guilty and went back to his chair. Ann grinned at the guilty schoolboy charm of his face.

"You'd better. Now, give the baby back to her father, and let me look you over, Ann."

Ann did as she was instructed and 30 minutes later,

Skye declared Ann fit to go home. "Between the robots, the drugs they used, and your own will, you're ready to go. But I'd say take a robot with you, Rager, just in case. I'll also be coming by daily to check on you both, at least until I'm satisfied that you're back to full health."

"That sounds like a good plan," Rager declared and looked at Ann with a huge grin. "I know one little puppy that's going to be very happy to see you."

"Poor Katy! Who's been taking care of her?" Ann asked as she realized she had a lot of questions. Too many to be sent off home with a baby she had no clue how to raise.

"Your mom for the most part, but she's been here with you a time or two. She's at home right now, the staff are looking after her."

"That's good." She said it softly and looked down at her now empty hands. "What do we feed the baby?"

"Your breastmilk," Skye said bluntly. "We've been pumping it from you and feeding her with bottles. The medicines you're on don't cross into your breastmilk, apparently, so we've been giving her that."

"Oh, that's why they ache now then?" Ann had noticed it but hadn't wanted to complain. Not when everyone had been so worried about her for so long.

"Yes, it's near to the time when we'd put the pumps on you." Skye looked a little uncomfortable talking about it, and Ann couldn't blame her, but it was still kind of funny to watch her friend squirm.

"So, you've been attaching pumps to my boobs, huh?" she asked when Rager walked out to find out where her parents were with her food. "You kinky little minx."

"Oh, stop it. It wasn't like that. I knew you'd tease me!" Skye glared at her but ruined it by laughing. "You do have nice breasts, but you're not my kind of girl, I'm afraid, Ann. You're more like a sister…"

"Damn! Friend-zoned by the only lesbian I know!" Ann felt a giggle bubbling up inside and knew that life would be different now. She'd almost died, and the impact of that hadn't fully hit her just yet. But she did know that teasing Skye was one thing she'd have to do more often. The way Skye blushed was cute, and despite the teasing, it made her smile. Ann suspected because it made her feel accepted. She hoped, anyway, maybe she was making one huge mistake, but Skye seemed to have a good reaction to it.

"Yep, and you'll stay there, missy. Even with those perfect breasts! I mean, it's lame that you're straight, but whatever." She winked, kissed Ann on the cheek, and then walked out of the room.

Ann was alone for the first time since she woke up. She needed to pee, she was still thirsty, and she was starving. But everyone had left the room to do something that meant she was being cared for. She'd almost died. The weight of it slowly sank over her, a fraction at a time.

Stella would have been without a mother. Rager without his soul mate. Her parents without their daughter. It would have rippled through this new world they wanted to build and darkened it for them all. Stella would have grown up without her.

All because of Rex and the stupid idea that he could make her belong to him. She hated him. She hated him more than she'd ever hated anyone. Her fists curled until her nails bit into her palms and she decided she would have to let go of this anger. It wasn't healthy, it could consume her. Or she could focus on her family and keeping them safe.

She'd talk to Rager, find out for sure what had happened to him, and if he wasn't gone, ask Rager to send him far, far away, where he could never find his way back. She had a family now, and she didn't want Rex to be anywhere near any of them ever again. If she had to be brutal to do that, so be it. She would do anything for those she loved.

Rager came back in quickly, gave her Stella, and smiled. "He's gone. He won't be back. He's on a planet so far away you don't even know it exists."

"Good, but how did you know what I was thinking about?"

"I could feel your anger." He opened a glass bottle filled with orange juice and handed it to her.

"Eek! Sorry." She took the bottle and guzzled it down.

"No, it's good, healthy. You're going to through a lot of emotions in the next few weeks, but I'll be there for you. You aren't alone, and never will be again."

"I love you, Rager," Ann said, just because she wanted to say it once again.

"I love you, Ann, forever."

20

Five Years Later

"It's amazing, isn't it?" Ann asked from her seat in the backyard of the building used as headquarters for the government of the sector now. She stared up at a second mothership, one that hovered close to the first one that came to the Earth five years ago. "It's going to Europe in a week, to begin projects there."

"Wow. I'd like to go with them. I always wanted to go to Europe," Skye said from the seat beside her. Ann's two small children, Stella and Anthony, ran around the playground set up for all children of government personnel.

"I heard they may take some of us with them. If you want, I can find out?" She looked over at her friend, still amazed after all these years, at just how beautiful the woman was.

"Maybe. I've trained a few more medics that could take my place for a little while." Skye had seemed restless lately and a little unhappy. A trip like that might be just what the other woman needed.

"I'll look into it for you." The first transporter came down and the women gathered the children up to take them inside.

A nanny came out of hiding and took over the care of the two children, so Skye and Ann walked up to the entrance hall. Ann nudged at Katy, still in her pocket, and smiled. The dog would never get tired of sleeping on Ann. Even when she'd been pregnant with Stella and Anthony, Katy still liked her daytime naps to be somewhere on Ann.

"We've made this a good world," Skye said out of the blue and Ann turned to look at her.

"What brought that on?" Ann asked, curious.

"All of this." She waved her hands around, and Ann looked at the gaily decorated entrance hall. "We've put up welcome signs and have all these activities planned for these new aliens coming in. Ten years ago, we'd have all been running in fear."

"Ten years ago we were too busy trying to survive," Ann reminded her friend. "But yeah, you're right. The government would have tried to blast them out of the sky and there would have been a very short-lived war that could have made this all go very differently."

"We still have problems. That lunatic out in Texas wants to bring slavery back." Skye said, as if she wanted to remind herself that this new world wasn't perfect.

"He's not gaining any ground, though, and if he makes too much trouble, Rager will take care of him." Ann had learned over time that Rager would listen to her, and when she heard news about men like this one, she passed it on to her mate. He would take care of it, and eliminate the problem.

Word had started to spread throughout the population of survivors that this was a new world and bullshit from the past wouldn't stand for long. Not long at all.

"I was glad he took out that place down in Mexico, where the women were being taken." That was Skye's polite way of saying a human sex trafficker had been caught. That man, and his crew, were all sent off-planet.

It was a punishment for those that committed the worst crimes, and was worse than death from what Ann understood. She didn't, couldn't feel bad for these people, women or men, that committed such terrible atrocities. She had a feeling the man in Texas would be the next one sent off-planet. It seemed some people just couldn't help themselves, and wanted to make others suffer for their own gain.

That idea had ruled the world for at least 2,000 years,

if not more. Those at the top would reap the rewards of those that labored below. It didn't fly in this world. You could profit, but your workers had to as well, and the ultimate goal was to ensure that everyone had exactly what they wanted. There were fewer people in the world now, it was possible to have all that you desired, within reason. As long as it didn't break the new laws of this brand new world.

"Hi, babe. Glad you made it." Rager interrupted her thoughts, and Ann's face lit up with pleasure.

"Hi there, yourself, handsome." She leaned up to kiss him and brushed at his cheek. "Always so breath-taking you."

"If you say so. How are the kids?"

"Fine, they're with Angela." She'd asked the woman to work for her after Anthony was born. Between her work with Rager, work at the medical clinic, and the hospital, Ann now had to spend a lot of time away from home. She hated it, but Angela helped, and she brought the kids with her when she could. It was a compromise she'd made,in order to take part in this experimental new world she'd helped to create.

"Good. Here they come." Rager spoke softly, and Ann inspected him.

He stood proudly, his face smooth, his eyes clear, and his body still in top condition. He wore one of the usual uniforms of the alien race, all black, but clean and neatly pressed. He didn't look the old world's version of a ruler or a king, but he did look like he meant business. Ann's heart fluttered as she looked at him, the passion still there, even after two kids and five years.

His hand reached out for hers, and she went to stand beside him. She was dressed in a simple black dress, made of t-shirt material, that flowed down to her ankles. It had long sleeves that covered her hands up to her fingers, and she felt like she presented a proper image to these newcomers. She was down to earth, but a professional, that should be taken seriously.

She'd studied hard with baby Stella at her side, and she'd become a medic right alongside Meg. She wasn't quite a doctor, that would still take more study, but she was as close as any of them were now. She was proud of what she'd achieved and had earned the respect of those around her ten times over.

Ann was jerked out of her thoughts by a noise at the doors. The doors came open and she could see a long line of people that waited to get into the building. Two men came in, one of whom looked a lot like Rager, but smaller.

"My youngest brother," Rager whispered down to her when she looked over at him in surprise. "His name is Thadeon. A bit of a scamp, but he means well. He's going to work in Europe with Melvenon there in the front."

"I see," she said softly, and waited for the rest to come in. Another group of men, soldiers with a high rank, and then a woman.

"My youngest sister. Her name is Athera. She's staying here, with us, to instruct us on new medical equipment she's brought with her."

"Oh. Skye, did you hear that?" Ann turned to see that Skye hadn't heard because she was too busy staring at Rager's sister.

The woman was tall, as tall as Rager, with long black hair tied in braids down her back, with glittering eyes a lighter shade of Rager's orange. She wore the customary uniform of Rager's people, but it was obvious the woman had a body that deserved to be painted. Slim, fit, with curves in all the right places, Ann could see why Skye was so… enraptured.

Ann smiled and nudged Rager. He looked down and smirked with satisfaction when he saw Skye's face. "I knew this might happen. My sister doesn't care for men in her bed. I thought she might make a good mate for your friend."

"Our friend!" Ann pointed out, but did it with a pleased smile. "Thank you."

"My pleasure, now, let's welcome the newcomers."

Ann did as was expected, but she kept an eye on Skye. The other woman skirted around Athera, made eye contact occasionally, but didn't quite have the courage to introduce herself yet. Skye had been alone for five long years, Ann knew, so it must be exciting to have this happen.

Ann had learned a lot about the mating phenomenon in the last few years. Some mates were joined together out of expedience and muddled along together. Others were soulmates, meant to be, and would be drawn together, no matter what. Ann had a suspicion this was the case for Skye and Athera.

She was pondering how imperfect the world was as Rager spoke with his younger brother a few hours later. There'd been a few more battles as men determined to make others their subjects fought the aliens that they could not defeat. Their efforts were misguided in their notions that they could defeat the aliens, that would never happen. It was impossible.

Their desire to subjugate others was just evil, and Rager and Ann, along with others, worked hard to root out the last of the resistance, and the few people that tried to build their own little kingdoms. They could not police the entire world, so there might be places where people lived in slavery, but not in this part of the planet.

That was the reason the newcomers had arrived. Even back then the aliens had known they'd need to bring more people over. Ann was glad they were there and that they would be on the other side of the planet, ensuring that the ideals and hopes of this side of the world were carried across.

"She's worked up her nerve," Rager said as he slipped up next to her and whispered in her ear.

"Oh my. I see she has." Ann glanced over where Athera and Skye were eyeing each other up, exchanging a word or two. "Two warriors, preparing for battle. Why can't they just say hello?"

"I think Skye had a rough life before she came here. Your world was cruel in a lot of ways to people like her. As for Athera, that's just how she is. Everything has to be a battle with her." Rager smiled, and she saw something in his eyes that looked like mischief. "I think they'll be at war for the rest of their lives, but look at how they look at each other. They'll fight to the death for the right to be together every day."

"That will suit Skye just fine, I think." Ann chuckled and looked away from the couple. "I'm glad we aren't like that though."

"No." Rager came even closer until her back was up against the wall and her eyes stared straight into his. "I'd much rather fuck you than fight you."

A shiver ran through her, a memory of pleasure he'd given her a thousand times, but still never grew old. "You'd better. I'm a much better lover than I am a warrior."

"That you are, my dear." He nuzzled her neck in the

dark corner where they were hidden, but then he let her go with regret in his eyes. "We have duties to attend to. But we will continue this discussion later."

She put her hand in his and they walked out of the corner, their heads high as they continued to circulate with the crowd. Ann met a lot of new faces, some that would go off to the other side of the world, and some that would stay with them. She tried to remember them all, but it became a jumble after a while.

Later, at dinner, she saw that Skye and Athera sat next to each other, but they both spoke to the people beside them, rather than to each other. It would come together, in time, she thought. It was fascinating to watch.

Ann looked around and caught a flash of light outside. Rain had returned quickly to the planet and along with it, storms. The lightning outside was just one more reminder that the world was getting back to normal. A good thing, in some ways.

"I want to take this moment to welcome you all to the new world, the new Earth. We are lucky that some of the people of this planet survived. With the help of Earth women, and the new women of our species we will rebuild this world for the children that we create. We have kept some of the ideas of the past, but some old ideas remain. You should all remember, as you take your new posts on this planet, that I am the leader of this entire planet. This is not our world, it's the world we are creating for our children. We should make it a place they can be proud of, and under my guidance, I know that's just what we'll create." Rager stood as the crowd in the dining hall clapped and murmured in approval. "Now, that's all the speech-making we'll have, if you don't mind. Please enjoy the rest of your evening."

"Not bad, Rager." Ann leaned over to whisper to her husband. "Short, to the point, and succinct."

"I hate long speeches," he replied, but then nuzzled her ear. "I have much better things to do with my mouth."

"That you do, and I do believe we'll be able to explore those things in about another hour." She turned with an intense heat in her own eyes, a heat only he could create. "It's 59 minutes too long, but I can wait."

"Well, if you're desperate, I can get started right now." His hand moved under the table to skim up her thigh until he found the center of heat he knew like the back of his own hand.

"I think I'd be too loud, right now. Save it for later." She kissed his cheek and he moved away with a disappointed frown. "I love you, you know."

"I love you too, Ann. More than I could ever explain." His eyes flared, and she felt him in that place inside of her that only he had ever occupied. That place around her heart where he lived as a warm part of her soul, a warmth that would never die. Her children had their own spots, but that one was only his.

With a last reluctant look, she went back to charming the older woman next to her, come to teach the earthlings about the planet that the aliens came from. It was part of the new curriculum at the schools they'd started for the children and coming children of the new world.

It was going to be a good place, for all of the new people of this Earth, Ann would make sure of it.

ABOUT THE AUTHOR

Selina Coffey is a romance writer who lives happily in London with her husband and son. She is a hopeless romantic who grew up always believing in love and she is not ashamed to admit this! It is this belief that makes her so passionate about writing crazy love stories.

A stereotypical girly girl, she loves shopping. So whenever she gets a chance and the spare cash, you will probably find her browsing online for the next pair of shoes to add to her collection!

You can find her online at
www.selinacoffey.com

Contact her at
hello@selinacoffey.com